# TH[E] Laundry Room PACT

*A Novel*

NIKKI LEIGH

VELVET
AFTER
DARK

VELVET AFTER DARK™

an imprint of Storyseed Press™,

a division of Storyseed Canada Limited

Published in Velvet paperback by Storyseed Canada Limited, 2025



velvetafterdark.ca

*Publisher's note: This book is a work of fiction. Names, characters, places and incidents either are the product of the author's imagination or are used fictitiously, and any resemblance to actual persons living or dead, events, or locales is entirely coincidental.*

LIBRARY AND ARCHIVES CANADA CATALOGUING IN PUBLICATION

Title: The laundry room pact : a novel / Nikki Leigh.

Names: Leigh, Nikki (Author of The laundry room pact), author.

Description: Series statement: Mom club confidential ; 1

Identifiers: Canadiana (print) 20250243342 | Canadiana (ebook) 20250244403

ISBN 9781997554189 (hardcover) | ISBN 9781997554165 (softcover) | ISBN 9781997554172 (EPUB)

Subjects: LCGFT: Novels.

Classification: LCC PS8623.E4742 L38 2025 | DDC C813/.6—dc23

Book formatting and

cover design by © Velvet After Dark™

VELVET AFTER DARK

WHERE STORIES STAY UP LATE WITH YOU

For the moms who weren't warned.
About the brain fog. The identity crisis.
The rage. The libido spike. The loneliness in a room full of people.
The way your body doesn't feel like yours—and then suddenly, wants everything at once.

You're not broken. You're just becoming.
And maybe you're finally asking for something that's only yours.

This one's for you.

There's still want.
Still fire.
*Still you.*

## Welcome to Mom Club Confidential

A series of spicy, emotionally messy love stories about the chaos of motherhood, the intimacy of long-term love, and the secrets women only share with each other—after bedtime, behind closed doors, and always with a group chat on fire.

Each book can be read as a standalone, but they're even more fun together.
This is just book **one**: The Laundry Room Pact.

Get ready to laugh, cry, and text your best friend,
"YOU NEED TO READ THIS."

# One

The dryer hums beneath her like white noise, like the monitors that used to buzz beside cribs. Soothing. Steady. A lullaby for a version of her that forgot she had a body beneath the exhaustion. It's the only sound left in the house—the low, steady lullaby of a life that used to be simpler. No monitors. No cries. No hands pulling at her. Claire closes her eyes and breathes in the silence. It's almost dangerous, the way she forgets to listen.

And that's when she feels him.

His chest presses against her back, and her body jolts before melting. The scent of him—clean sweat, laundry soap, and the ghost of a cologne he gave up years ago—wraps around her. He's heat and muscle and the grounding pull of something she forgot she needed. She doesn't think. She just leans back into him.

"You shouldn't have left this unlocked," Nate murmurs, his breath dragging across the shell of her ear.

"Maybe I didn't," she whispers, as his hand slides beneath her shirt.

His touch is rougher than memory, calloused fingers gliding up her stomach, the scrape of his thumb skimming under her bra. It makes her remember—the old spark, the car windows fogging up and stolen kisses in dark stairwells.

She shudders, electricity crackling through nerves long starved for it.

He lifts her tank top slowly, knuckles grazing sensitive skin. She's not sure whether he means to pull the shirt all the way off, but she raises her arms, offering it up like a question and answer. His mouth finds her neck as he slides the fabric over her head, and her entire body shudders, leaving her chest bare and wanting.

God, she missed this.

His hands find her bare breasts—softened by years of feeding, comforting, giving—cupping, kneading, thumbs flicking over sensitive nipples. Not the same as they once were. But still hers. Still his. Still capable of this sharp, electric hunger. Claire gasps, arching into him, and his groan rumbles through her. They follow the subtle slopes of her shoulders and the curves that soften with each year of marriage, each baby. He pulls her back into him, breath roughening as her body molds against his. She can feel him through her leggings, the hardness of him, the urgency she used to take for granted—back when they were young and reckless, before babies and exhaustion turned every touch into a negotiation of time and energy. Claire's pulse quickens, her chest rising and falling in shallow gasps.

"You don't even know what you do to me," he growls.

She barely registers when he hooks his thumbs into her leggings. She just lifts—offering herself up like a lamb, a dare, a desperate fucking hope—and he peels them down her hips, baring her ass to the cool air, to the heat of his gaze.

When she leans back, it's deliberate. Intimate. Her breathing is frantic as he kneels to slide the fabric the rest of the way down. He's always been practical—rarely on his knees for anything. But the sight of him now, barechested and rough around the edges, makes her forget every responsible, grounded reason they don't do this anymore.

Nate. Practical Nate.

Always moving fast, always doing what needed to be done.

Not tonight.

Tonight he's slow. Deliberate. Worshipful.

Nate spreads her legs with demanding hands, pushing the cloth just far enough down her thighs. His palms trail upward, spreading warmth as he moves. There's a brief, exquisite pause as his fingers reach her, as he hesitates, as if savoring the anticipation.

And then—

His fingers slide between her folds, slick and aching for him. He groans—a sound torn from somewhere low and starved.

"Fuck, Claire," he breathes.

She whimpers, helpless. His thumb circles her clit with devastating precision, feather-light at first, then harder, meaner, until her thighs start to tremble. His free arm wraps around her waist, holding her up, holding her down, pinning her against the counter like a secret he's afraid to lose.

"You're already shaking," he murmurs against her spine. "Forgot how sensitive you get."

She sobs—yes, yes—and he slides a finger inside, thick and slow. It's been years since she stretched for anyone but labor, anyone but pain. This? This is for her. For want. For want. The intrusion is too much and not enough. She rocks back, greedy, mindless.

"Just like that," he grits out. "Take me. Take everything."

Claire can't speak. She can barely breathe. She's a trembling, gasping wreck against the counter, held together only by his hands and the rhythm he builds inside her—stretch, press, circle, thrust. Nate curls his finger inside her and she breaks open—head dropping, body clenching, pleasure sparking like live wires under her skin.

"You're so fucking beautiful when you lose control," he whispers.

She tries to answer but all that comes out is a broken whimper. A plea. Another finger joins the first, forcing her to stretch, to take more. She sobs into the counter, clawing at the laminate, body greedy for the pressure, burn, breathtaking fullness.

"Gonna watch you fall apart on my hand, Claire," he growls, voice thick and raw. "Gonna make you forget every goddamn thing but me."

And God help her—she already has.

Nate's fingers drive into her again—slow, unrelenting—until Claire is nothing but open nerve endings and wrecked breathing. She clutches the counter, hips grinding back helplessly, chasing every flick of his thumb, every stretch of his fingers.

He doesn't let up.

Doesn't let her hide in comfort.

He wants her undone.

"So tight," he grits against her ear, voice frayed with awe and filthy affection. "Gonna stretch you open, sweetheart. Gonna make you remember what it's like to be full of me."

She gasps, frantic, every muscle straining to take more. Her thighs shake. Her calves burn. Her heart pounds so loudly she thinks it might crack her chest wide open. He thrusts his fingers deeper, scissoring slightly, opening her up inch by devastating inch. Claire cries out, shameless now, every thrust punching a sound out of her throat she doesn't recognize.

"You feel this?" he growls.

"You feel how fucking desperate you are for me?"

She nods—wild, frantic—and he withdraws his fingers.

For a heartbeat, she's empty. Cold. Starving.

And then—

The thick head of his cock nudges against her slick entrance, and Claire sobs aloud, hips canting back, trying to take him before he even lets her.

"Goddamn," Nate hisses, gripping her hips hard enough to bruise. "You're fucking soaked for me."

He doesn't tease. Doesn't ease.

He pushes inside her in one long, brutal stroke—splitting her open, making her body stretch and clutch around him with a raw, helpless moan.

"Fuck, Nate—" she gasps, wrecked, forehead dropping to the counter.

"That's it," he snarls, driving deeper until he's seated fully inside her, balls pressed against the backs of her thighs.

"Take it all, Claire. Take every fucking inch."

She is.

God, she is.

She can feel every pulsing beat of him buried inside her. The thick, overwhelming stretch of him fills every desperate, lonely inch she forgot she had. He pulls out slow, cruel, before slamming back in. Punishing. Perfect. Her cry breaks open against the counter. The sound of their bodies slapping together fills the laundry room, dirty and raw and real.

"You're mine," he rasps, hips slamming into her ass. "You hear me? Fucking mine."

"Yours," she sobs. "Always—"

He wraps a fist in her hair, yanking her head back so he can bite down on the curve of her neck, marking her, owning her. Claire shatters against him—body clenching, spasming, desperate for the orgasm coiling at the base of her spine. Every thrust drives her closer. Every filthy word he snarls against her skin wrecks her a little more.

"God, look at you," he groans. "Fucking trembling for it. Begging for it. You're gonna come so hard, you won't even remember your own goddamn name."

She whimpers, thighs shaking—like holding up toddlers, groceries, too many years without letting herself fall apart. And now she's falling. Letting herself be caught.

"I can feel you, Claire," he groans, pounding into her harder, rougher. "So fucking tight. So close. Come for me, baby. Let me feel you fall apart."

And she does—with a broken, ragged scream she can't hold back if she tried.

Her whole body clenches down around him, spasming in frantic waves that have her sobbing his name, scrabbling for purchase, mind completely blank except for the burn and the bliss and NateNateNate.

He curses, slams into her once, twice, and then he's spilling inside her with a wrecked groan, pulsing deep, grinding into her like he never wants to let her go.

They collapse against the counter—still tangled, still gasping, still connected by something way deeper than skin. Nate's forehead presses to the back of her shoulder, his breathing harsh against her damp skin.

Neither of them speaks. Silence used to mean something wrong—crying monitors, slammed doors, exhaustion thick enough to drown in. This silence is different. This silence holds her.

✒

The world blurs into sensation.

Claire's forehead presses against the counter, her body trembling, thighs slick and aching, still clenching helplessly around the thick, fading pulse of him inside her.

Nate doesn't move.

He stays buried deep, breathing harsh and uneven against her shoulder, like he can't bring himself to let go. The dryer hums beneath them—

steady, indifferent, as if it hasn't just witnessed her being wrecked from the inside out.

Claire floats in the aftermath, drunk on the feeling of him still pulsing inside her, on the heat and the ache and the raw, impossible fullness that nothing else in her life touches.

Nate shifts just enough to press a kiss between her shoulder blades—gentle, grounding—and it guts her more than any thrust. She reaches for him blindly, sliding one hand back, needing to feel him, anchor herself to the reality of this moment. His fingers lace through hers, squeezing once, rough and sure.

The smallest thing—and it undoes her. Tears burn at the back of her throat, not from sadness but from the unbearable, breakable tenderness of it.

Of him still here.

Of her still his.

She closes her eyes and lets herself drown in it—the press of his body, the scent of their sweat and soap and skin, the delicious soreness blooming between her thighs. There's no rush to clean up. No scramble to redress. No shame.

Just this.

Just them.

Held together for once by something more than exhaustion or obligation or schedules. Held together by the desperate, aching need to find their way back. And for the first time in what feels like forever, Claire doesn't think about tomorrow.

For once, she doesn't have to get up. Doesn't have to clean, fix, soothe. For once, she can just let herself be held. And she stays.

# Two

Claire wakes in bed—wet, wanting, and alone.

The edge of a dream fading to a warm and humiliating blur. Her heart thuds. Her shirt sticks damp to her skin. She tugs it away, shifting beneath the covers, feeling alone even with Nate's body beside her. The memories stretch into waking like claw marks.

Fucking wild.

Biting the sheets.

She aches with the shame of it, trying to steady her breath. Trying to understand this want inside her. The soft sounds of the house waking up drown her attempts at remembering more. Damp hair and cereal and the never-ending loop of Goldfish and YouTube. Their mornings all go like this: over-scheduled and underwater. So why can't she shake the heat from her skin, even as the kids start to stir?

Upstairs, a thump and the baby's muffled wail send her slipping out of bed. She winces as she stands, shifting uncomfortably. The ache lingers beneath reality, quiet but insistent. She pauses in the hallway, trying to breathe, touching the edge of her shirt like it might burn. Across from her, the kids' door creaks open, and she sees her oldest buried in stuffed animals. He doesn't notice her yet. His voice rises, clear and small. "Heathie, you woke up too loud." Claire blinks, trying to focus. Trying to slide back into mom mode. She watches them move around the room, jumbled curls and footed pajamas, her body hot and weightless, as if she were floating in a strange new world. Her three-year-old joins the chorus with a long whimper, and she knows this is a countdown until chaos.

She peeks her head in. "Socks on, guys! Breakfast is almost ready!"

"Boo cereal!" says the three-year-old. "I want choco toast!"

The baby stands in his crib, tears evaporating as he catches sight of her. She swoops him up, inhaling his sleep-sweet head, bouncing him gently as he wraps both arms around her neck. He mumbles happily into her shoulder. She closes her eyes, leaning into him, letting herself be anchored. Letting herself forget how long and lonely the nights feel. But as soon as she steps away from the door, he's squirming to get down, wriggling with toddler determination. Her shirt rides up as she puts him on the floor, and a flush rises on her neck at the memory of needing so much. Needing Nate's hands and mouth and fingers everywhere.

She follows them down the hall, still damp, still unsteady, and peeks into the bathroom. Her reflection startles her. Is that heat or exhaustion across her cheeks? She sighs and strips off the shirt, running cold water across her wrists and looking at the circles beneath her eyes. Would Nate see this version of her if he ever looked? Would he know what she needed, even now? She takes her time toweling off, opening the medicine cabinet, running fingertips over a box she hasn't touched since baby number three. Her breath catches as she remembers the dream—lube and slick and desperate—and then she slams it shut.

The house is too quiet. They must be raiding the pantry already, spilling Cocoa Puffs and whining for apple juice. Her need is a dull hum beneath the familiar noise, like she can't quite make sense of herself, like she isn't awake enough to want so much. She finds a tank top and pulls it over her head, then wiggles into jeans that are soft from wear but still snug on her hips. They remind her how different her body used to be. How much he used to love peeling clothes away. She forces herself to step back into the hallway, braless and distracted, swallowing the knot in her throat.

By the time she reaches the kitchen, the kids have emptied the pantry. Her seven-year-old stands on the table like he's won a treasure hunt, grinning with proud mischief. Claire is still lightheaded and half-gone. How can they need so much when she feels so empty? Her middle child circles the chairs, arms out like an airplane. She wants to sink into her own thoughts, escape to a time when mornings didn't feel like drowning. When Nate looked at her like he couldn't wait to come home. She leans against the counter and closes her eyes, desperate to recapture the warmth that pulsed through her just hours ago. But her toddler's whining drags her back to the surface.

"Mama! Cereal! Milk!"

Heath is on the floor, shaking a box upside down and catching stray puffs in his fists. Claire opens her eyes to an exploded-bomb mess, more chaos than she can handle. She picks up the baby, scattering cereal with her toes, and heads for the fridge. They're both clinging now, the baby to her hip and her body to its unshakable heat. The oldest stretches out a long, accusatory syllable. "Moo-oom." He drops his bowl on the table and crosses his arms, serious. "You forgot to do breakfast again."

"Don't let him shake the box," Claire mutters, balancing on one leg as she snatches it back. She pries a bowl off the stack and flinches as it clatters onto the table. Too many noises. Too many needs. Too little of herself left. The boys crowd her, all sticky hands and bony knees, and Claire watches from outside her own body as it juggles and reaches and picks the right-colored cups. Her seven-year-old catches the look on her face and squints, trying to place it.

"Are you sad?" he asks.

"Just tired," Claire murmurs. She sets the milk on the table, lets them wrestle over it, and finally slides into a chair. Lets herself unravel, just a little. "Tired" doesn't come close to what she is. "Tired" isn't a good enough reason to ache all over.

She breathes deep and steady. It's her most convincing show of control. She's mom. She's wife. She's got this. But then her foot squelches on something sticky, and Claire gasps. The whole morning unravels like the day before it, and the day before that, an endless thread of mess and noise and chaos, and she wants so much to pull it taut. The baby drops a banana, and she feels the smushed mush under her toes, inescapable. She sighs and wipes her foot on her jeans, imagining herself alone and wild, hair pulled and clothes torn and need twisting sharp through her.

She lets out a long breath and grips the table's edge. "I want to go back to bed."

"Again?" says her oldest, rolling his eyes.

He finally notices. His frown lands like an insult: not want, not hunger—just disapproval. "You need to put a shirt on."

"I need a lot of things," Claire mumbles.

But no one is listening. Not even Nate. He's appeared at the kitchen door, hair damp and curls wild from his own shower, ready to step into the chaos that used to overwhelm him.

He's already dressed for work, her blue-collar husband in a crisp grey shirt and jeans, clean and fresh and totally unfazed. His attention flicks to the floor, the table, the half-open box of Cocoa Puffs, but it doesn't linger there. It doesn't linger anywhere. She wonders what he sees, if it still feels worth coming home to.

"You forgot to clean," says the oldest, always eager to help point things out.

He jumps up and down, gesturing dramatically at the floor, and Claire's need gets pushed deeper beneath the surface.

Nate gives them a tired smile and tosses them a promise she knows he won't keep: "I'll clean up when I get home."

Heath watches with wide eyes, repeating his favorite word: "Home. Home. Home."

And then he dumps a new box of cereal on his head.

"Aw, man," says Nate, tucking keys and a packed lunch into his pockets. "Good luck with that."

She tries to pretend she isn't overwhelmed. "I think we both need it," she says.

Her voice wobbles, a little sharper than intended. Nate's gaze finally settles on her, slow and careful, landing on a piece that's too small for him to notice. She watches him observe the outline of her unbrushed hair, the circles under her eyes, the flush of her cheeks. He doesn't see the heat or the need, doesn't know how wrecked she feels.

"Hang in there," he says, his voice softening.

He comes closer, careful around the crushed cereal, and she tips her chin toward him. Her eyes flick to his mouth, to the dark scruff on his jaw. She remembers the weight of him, the urgency in his kiss when they couldn't keep their hands off each other. Back before this. Back before all of this. He leans in and plants one on her forehead, his gesture quick and automatic. A morning routine. A way of saying I'm still here but only barely.

She lifts her hand, a small wave. "Bye," she says.

"Bye, Dad," echoes the three-year-old.

The baby adds his own chirpy "Bye!"

Nate turns and opens the door, ducking out to the driveway and pausing for just a second before pulling it closed. Claire can almost see the life that waits for him: less chaotic, less claustrophobic, less like the mornings that leave her wanting to escape into her own world. She wraps her arms around herself, trying to feel the warmth he left behind, trying to remember when she felt steady and strong. It's not enough. It's never enough.

"Bye, babe," he calls from the driveway, and she watches him walk to the car.

It feels like they're a million miles apart.

She breathes in deep and shaky. Stares at the door like he's still there, still looking at her. But he's not. Claire feels the weight of what they used to be. She imagines mornings with less mess, less noise, more of the two of them than the thousand other things that fill their lives. The things that fill his life, too, no matter how much she hopes he's as wrecked by this as she is.

She stares at the door. It doesn't make her feel less alone.

It doesn't make her want any less.

✒

The day spins like the words on a dryer cycle: delicate, heavy-duty, low-heat, cold-rinse. Claire is caught between a high spin and a hard place, still craving the dream, its ache soaking into everything she does. The morning fades to afternoon, laundry tumbling, phone buzzing, baby on her hip. The kids smear their lunch as her mind loops.

It was so vivid. It felt so fucking real. She needs to be taken again, filled, bent over, wanting. By the time she sits alone, the laundry folded and the baby finally asleep, Claire can't resist the urge to write it down: Bent over the dryer, his fingers everywhere. I begged him without a sound.

The want lingers like a haunting. She's hungry for more than Nate's goodbye, for more than his kiss on the forehead. The house is a minefield of reminders, triggering the wild need she can't shake. It was only a dream. But even now, her thighs clench remembering the moment before she woke. The air feels sticky as she moves through the house. She finds a juice cup behind the couch, soggy Goldfish in the carpet, endless traces of the kids in every room. Their mess is a flood that rises around her, reality refusing to let her surface. She closes her eyes as she hears their familiar demands. As her heart thuds with less familiar ones. *Bent over the dryer, his fingers everywhere.*

Her hand flies to her chest. Her pulse is frantic beneath it. Her thoughts spin fast, her mind spiraling through moments she can't explain. She tosses toys in a bin, picks up an abandoned sock, watches the kids argue over blocks. Her head feels like it's on a hinge, attached to her body but floating away. She's shaky and damp, grasping at air and knowing the whole day will be like this. How did it leave her so raw? How did it cut so deep? Laundry detergent. Dryer hum. Counter. Clothes. Toys. Even the kids pulling at her sends her body into overload. Every ordinary thing is a reminder, a shock, a trap. The more she tries to ignore it, the more she needs him. Needs to be filled, needs to be fucked, needs to be taken apart. She moves through the hours, trying to hold herself together, feeling heat seep into her skin.

"Mama! Watch!"

She jumps, and it jars her loose.

The three-year-old grins up at her, eyes wild. He stacks blocks with his older brother, oblivious to how gone she is. Her breath is caught, and she can barely exhale. She forces her eyes open, looking at their eager faces. Trying to stay present. Trying to care.

"You gotta see this, Mom!"

"I'm looking, guys," Claire lies.

She's always "looking" and "listening" and "almost done" with whatever is just a distraction. She's good at pretending she's in the moment, even when the truth is stamped like a silent tattoo across her skin. The hum of the dryer comes from the hallway, low and thick and teasing. It gets her every time, so much that she can't think straight, can't walk a single step without remembering how his body held her still. She turns to the boys, and her voice doesn't sound like hers. "I'll be right back. Gotta change the laundry."

She shuts the door behind her and stands frozen in the sound of clothes spinning. Her pulse is a hard, relentless throb. She rests one hand on top of the dryer, feeling it vibrate through her fingertips. Feeling it everywhere. She gasps and yanks her hand back, staring at the shaking machine, the barely shut door. The need is raw and undeniable. It's pushing at her insides, so big it feels like she'll never escape. Her knees are weak. Her breath catches. She falls against the wall, alone with this reckless longing, trying to make sense of how her body responds. The sounds of the house blur and buzz like static. She can only hear her own thudding heart, her own desperate need, growing so loud that she can't ignore it. She slides to the floor and closes her eyes, biting her lip to stop herself from crying out. She feels it everywhere.

Everywhere.

It doesn't stop. Not for a second. The chaos builds, and she can't get herself under control. It winds through every room, more mess, more toys, more reminders that the day will never end. That the heat won't fade. The boys have moved on from their block tower, asking for mac-and-cheese, jumping off the couch, wanting more and more of her. She can't even pretend to keep up. She can't even remember how. The dream blurs with reality, teasing her with echoes. It felt so fucking real. She holds her body still, expecting the ache to fade, but it never does. She opens her eyes and looks at the noise of life around her, knowing it's like this for Nate, too. How can it not be, when they used to be so close?

*The words repeat in her mind. Bent over the dryer. His fingers everywhere.*

She looks up to find her oldest staring at her like she's a science project gone wrong.

"Mom, you're spacing."

"Sorry, buddy."

Claire exhales slowly and holds her arms out to him.

"Come here, you two."

Heath yelps "ME!" and runs, quick and wobbly, to reach her first.

The three-year-old isn't far behind, launching himself into her lap with dramatic flair. They are all elbows and knees, jabbing into her sides. They feel it, even if they can't name it. They know she's somewhere else. They know she needs to be wrecked. They pile onto her like they'll bring her back to life, and the mess of them keeps her just grounded enough. Just barely in this world. They stay there for a while, sitting on the floor, toys and laundry scattered around them. Claire wraps them in her arms, pulling them close, knowing her body will never keep up with her mind. Knowing they can never hold her tight enough.

The chaos fades to a manageable buzz, and Claire drags herself up, pulling the kids along with her. The older boys settle into a video, and she gives them an extra half-hour of screen time as a gift to herself. Just this once. Just today. She watches them go slack-jawed in front of the TV. She watches the toddler smear his face with applesauce, then grabs him a yogurt for good measure. He tosses the spoon to the floor and digs in with both hands, cheeks sticky and stained. She's resigned to the mess. She's resigned to everything. When the yogurt's half gone, he gives her the last spoonful, and she knows it's the biggest sacrifice a one-year-old can make. She swallows it down with a smirk. Then she scoops him up, kisses the top of his head, and wraps him in a half-clean blanket, humming under her breath as he nuzzles into her chest. He's asleep before she gets halfway through his usual lullaby.

Her mind races as she carries him upstairs. Her body remembers everything. She feels the heat pool and pulse through her. She needs to write it down, get it out, capture the wanting. She needs it so bad she might burst. Claire moves quietly through the hallway, clutching the baby close, trying not to wake him with the urgency in her chest. Bent over. Begging. Silent. His fingers everywhere.

The house presses in—silence too thick, air too still. Even empty rooms seem to watch her. She puts the baby in his crib and watches him snuggle his stuffed rabbit, a small bundle of sleep and need. He reminds her of Nate, in a way. Messy hair, stubborn will. Less needy than he should be.

Claire tucks the blanket around him and presses her palm to his back, the weight of her hand so gentle and soft. "Night-night," she whispers, kissing his cheek.

She closes the door slowly, easing herself back to the landing. Her heart drums against her ribs, frantic and full of heat. She tries to stay steady. Tries not to explode.

The boys are still wrapped up in their show, half-aware of their own little world. She listens from the stairs, hearing only their soft laughter and the gentle hum of animation. Claire takes her chance. She picks up her phone and slinks to the kitchen, where the butcher-block counter waits for her. She leans on it, feeling the edge against her spine, holding her weight with both hands. It's too close, too much, and she arches her back in a way that pulls a whimper from her lips. The dream is all over her skin, sharp and hot and impossible to ignore.

Claire finally sags against the counter, clutching her phone, scrolling aimlessly through apps. Trying to ignore the way her body winds tighter, the way her need refuses to unwind. But her finger hovers. Stops. Reverses. She bites her lip, wondering if she has the nerve, wondering if she'll explode, wondering if it's enough.

She taps on the Notes app, quick and reckless. Breath catching, heart thudding, so fucking hot and so alone. She taps until the letters feel like touches. Until the touches make her shiver. She writes it all down:

*Bent over the dryer, his fingers everywhere. I begged him without a sound.*

Her hands are shaky as she reads it back, breathless and exposed. The words burn into her skin, and the heat makes her dizzy. Her mind spins. Her whole world spins. Even the floor seems to spin beneath her. She types a quick, trembling title: Grocery List.

✒

She locks the note with a passcode. Holds her breath as she stares at it. Then, like the weight of it all is too much to bear, she sinks to the ground with her head between her knees. The house spins. The dream won't leave. She sits on the cold tile, dizzy with need—still unsure if it's desire or grief.

# Three

Claire stares at the screen in shock. What? Still no idea how they always know. They have no idea. Yet they just know.

Mom Club Confidential

Mon, Mar 4 at 12:25 PM

Harper

how many times do you have to fantasize about your husband before it counts as cheating

Naomi

that depends—

are you bent over the dryer or the butcher block?

The whining starts before she reaches the top step. Claire isn't sure if it's Jamie or her own voice—two kids wanting two different things and only one exhausted mother to give them both. Her arms are filled with laundry and discarded baby toys. Her head is filled with the chaos of the last two hours. Jamie wants the red water bottle. Lila wants the pink one.

They all want more of her than she has left to give. She drops the clothes in a heap by the door and takes a deep breath before venturing into the tangled mess of bedtime. She finds it where she left it, except worse.

Lila sits cross-legged on the top bunk, tangled curls hanging over her eyes, mismatched pajamas half on and half off. She's rubbing her eyes and wailing, full volume, like she's just been told dessert is a myth and sugar never existed. Her red water bottle—Lila's, not Jamie's, though Claire can barely keep track—is leaking onto the carpet. Jamie watches it with quiet satisfaction. Too quiet. If she's learned anything as a mom, it's that silence and children don't go together. It means something is wrong. It means someone is up to something, and that someone is usually her middle child.

"Jamie, what are you—"

The soft sound of a page-turning draws her attention to the other side of the room. There, Claire sees a tiny smirk playing at the corners of his not-so-innocent mouth. She'd laugh if she wasn't already teetering on the edge of frustration. If she hadn't already picked up the same crumpled water bottle three times tonight. Instead, she lets out a slow breath. "Jamie, we don't read Lila's bedtime stories until we're all tucked in. Remember?"

"But I want the blue cup!" His smirk fades, replaced by the same wide-eyed desperation as his older sister.

Claire closes her eyes and imagines a bubble bath, a locked door, a world where toddlers don't gang up on their parents. She also imagines another round of bickering, sibling squabbles, and three over-tired kids. She knows which one she'll be getting.

It's another hour before she finishes. One more rocking chair marathon, one more request for water, one more lap around the house to make sure the front door is locked. Nate would usually do it, but she can hear the water running upstairs. They're both exhausted. Too exhausted to even split the routine. She rubs her temples, debates putting a pot of coffee on and pushing through her headache.

Her phone buzzes with a message from the group chat:

Mom Club Confidential
Mon, Mar 4 at 7:12 PM

Naomi

Don't tell me you guys have the flu too.

Claire

Oh we do, all right.

Send help or send wine.

She's only half joking.

The kids start shrieking from the bathroom—something about a toothbrush in the toilet—and Claire tosses the phone onto the counter before it can buzz again.

Something catches her ankle on her way to the couch; she stumbles forward, narrowly avoiding a collision with the wall. She looks down at the half-built tower of blocks. Smiles at the cluttered mess and the chaos of family life. At least Jamie and Lila's fingerprints match the paint colors. Even when they're in trouble, they somehow get away with it. Even when they're driving her to the brink, she's still too soft to do anything but love them.

She picks up the blocks and stacks them in the overflowing toy bin, ignores the dusting of cracker crumbs that never seems to leave the carpet. Nate is still in the shower when she finally gives up and makes her way upstairs. She doesn't even turn the light off behind her. Doesn't bother with toys that will find their way underfoot again tomorrow. She steps over a lone sock in the hallway. Can't tell if it's Nate's or Lila's or Jamie's. Can't tell where her body ends and everyone else's needs begin. A shared space. A shared life. She doesn't regret any of it.

But it's also a shared exhaustion. And she doesn't know how long they can keep running like this. Doesn't know if he can still feel her reaching when he's too tired to do anything but close his eyes.

She catches a glimpse of herself in the hallway mirror, dark hair coming loose from a braid, the top of Nate's t-shirt falling over one shoulder. Her skin is still pale from winter, but there's a flush beneath the surface. It's like her body is catching up with the parts of her she tries to keep at bay. Like she's already half way to falling apart.

Maybe Nate doesn't notice, but she does. It's there when she pulls the clip from her hair, when she runs her fingers through the messy waves, when she lets out a shaky breath. A small crack that widens, softens, slowly splits. She hears him climb into bed as she turns off the shower. She takes one last look at the dark hallway behind her. Feels the pull of something she can't quite name. It's not hopelessness, but it's not hope. Not yet.

She crawls in next to him, heavy limbs and tired eyes, and sinks into the sheets. Feels the warmth of his body even though he's turned away, even though he's already halfway to sleep. It's not hopelessness, but it's not enough.

She wants more.

And she can't stop wondering if he does, too.

✒

The first time Nate's hand moves against her hip, Claire thinks she might have imagined it. An accident, she tells herself. She waits for him to settle back into sleep. He doesn't.

His grip tightens, a low heat against her skin. It's not the touch of an exhausted man reaching for contact before rolling over and drifting away. It's not an unconscious, habitual embrace before slipping into silence. She has spent too many nights tracing the contours of his shoulders, listening to the soft sounds of his breathing, pretending her own sighs weren't as heavy as they felt. She knows exactly what his indifference sounds like. But this time, it doesn't come.

Her eyes are still shut, but she doesn't need to see his face. She knows he's watching her. He can see the slight tremor in her lip as she bites down on it, unsure if it's real, afraid to even breathe in case it's not. It is. He's there, hovering close, tracing the familiar outline of her body like she's new and unknown. Like he's discovering her for the first time again.

Her own hand stays still, doesn't make a move toward him. Can't. Doesn't know what she'll do if he doesn't make the next move himself. For one long, breathless second, she thinks she'll have to. But his touch, hesitant and heated, starts to drift lower. She can't quite make out the sound of her own sigh beneath the rushing of her heart. She hears it anyway. A shaky, wanting sound.

His fingers hook under the waistband of her shorts, inch by inch, testing her, testing himself, slipping below. Her body responds before she can stop it, the familiar flutter of her pulse, the telling flush on her cheeks, the slow arch of her back as he holds her there, half-claimed, half-explored, on the verge of being someone he remembers.

She doesn't dare to move, and she doesn't dare to hope, but it becomes clear he's not asleep.

Not in the slightest.

✒

His hand dips lower. Claire can hardly breathe. He lets it linger against her thigh, teasing, deliberate, making her want him with more than her imagination.

Her hips tense beneath his touch, and for a moment she wonders if this will end like all the others: another half-asleep promise, another morning spent wondering if he even knows she's still here. Another lonely reach for something just out of grasp. She wonders, but not for long.

This time, his touch doesn't retreat.

She opens her eyes and finds him there. Watching. Awake and aware and exactly who she remembers. The grip of his hand is firmer now, the weight of it familiar and still new, even after all this time. He trails his fingers toward the center of her, leaving a hot, unrelenting line in their wake, the air around them charged with all the things they stopped saying.

Her own desire surges to the surface, doesn't hold back, doesn't need to. He moves above her, and she gives into the sensation of being full—of need, of longing, of him—before he even touches her. She feels his hard cock against the edge of her sleep shorts, feels him before she even feels him, a raw gasp catching in her throat, a soft sound giving away how ready she is, how much she's been holding back, how desperate she is to not hold back any longer.

Her muscles twitch beneath his touch, the familiar tension giving way to the beginning of something unfamiliar: surrender. It feels like he might let go again, might stop, might pull away. But he doesn't.

This time, Nate's grip is tight.

He dips beneath her waistband, finds her core, never breaking the steady heat of his gaze as she lets out a soft, telling moan. The sound he used to chase. The sound she used to beg for.

This time, he doesn't stop. He shifts, adjusting himself over her, and there's something playful in his expression, something determined and intense and unsaid. Claire isn't sure when she stopped believing this was possible. She only knows she wants to believe it now.

Another soft whimper escapes, but she doesn't dare to say more, doesn't want to break whatever spell is keeping them here. His fingertips draw circles against her, taunting and relentless, as though they have all the time in the world to remember each other's edges. But Claire doesn't. Her body, tense and waiting, won't let her pretend this is enough. Not anymore. Not after everything she's let herself want again.

Her breath comes in shallow bursts, pants, every part of her urging, begging, yielding. His fingers play at her entrance, skimming just shy of it, round back to spread her with just enough pressure to make her curse her own patience. It's been too long. They've been too far apart. She's tired of wanting without having. She's tired of staying quiet when she could be taken.

"Please." Her voice is barely a whisper, but he hears it. She knows he does.

It's all the permission he needs.

It's all the invitation he wants.

He slips a single, careful finger inside, feels the flutter and heat of her need wrapped around him, and his mouth hovers just close enough to brush against hers. She's close enough to catch his laugh, his breath, the low sound he makes just for her.

He moves again, but she holds him there, breathless and silent and far more commanding than she intends to be. Her small, fierce grip says it all: not this time, not yet, don't let go, don't you fucking dare.

*She remembers the way he used to touch her like this — like she was a promise, not a burden.*

✒

He shifts, pinning her with the weight of his body, the strength of his arms. Claire feels a dizzy, heated pull between wanting this to last forever and needing it now, needing it fast. Nate hovers above her, slow, deliberate, fingers still working her with an unbearable rhythm, bringing her close and then closer and then stopping just shy of the point she craves.

He knows how wet she is. She knows he's not going to let it end any time soon.

Another finger presses in, gentle at first, stretching, filling, making her gasp and arch her back. His movements are firm but tender, insistent, the way they used to be, the way she dreamed they would be again. He adds a small squeeze of lube, a slow, taunting slide that makes her tremble beneath him. He dips lower, hooking his fingers deeper inside, dragging her over the edge before pulling her back, giving her just enough to make her breathless, just enough to make her want more.

"Jesus, Claire."

He moves harder, quicker, almost losing control but still focused, still holding her there, still not letting her shatter. The rough timbre of his voice does something to her she can't name, something more intimate than a touch, more vulnerable than skin against skin.

"Look how close you are."

She almost comes at that alone. At the sound of it. At the fact that they're here, after all this time, after all the doubts, after all the nights they barely looked at each other. He looks at her now, so intently, so unapologetically, as she twists and moans and grips him even tighter. She can barely form a coherent thought, let alone words, but she doesn't have to. Her body says everything, each desperate movement a demand she used to hold back, each silent plea a confession she thought she'd forgotten how to make.

He adjusts, shifting the weight of his body and the focus of his fingers, a low groan escaping his throat as she clenches tighter, wetter, and gasps his name. The pressure is relentless. The stretch of his fingers and the heat of his body, her world reduced to this small, raw, dizzying point of want. The heat of it. The fullness. The way he's completely there with her. She rides the edge of exhaustion and ecstasy, feels the buzz of their oldest baby monitor from the next room over, knows it's not a match for the sound of them. It was never a match for the sound of them.

"Don't stop. Oh god. Don't—"

Her eyes squeeze shut, breathless, trembling, holding onto the pillow and to him and to the shreds of herself as she teeters on the brink, closer, closer, closer. "—fucking stop."

He doesn't.

Not until he feels her pulling him back, grounding him with the pressure of her hand on his cock, reminding him that they have nowhere to be, nothing to prove, no need to rush. Not until her frantic grip draws his focus away from watching her come completely undone.

She hears him groan, feels him twitch against her palm, a low, hungry noise that makes her insides ache and tighten. It's his turn to shiver. It's his turn to remember that they're both so close, both so unguarded, both so undone.

"Fuck, Claire."

His head dips against her shoulder, then back up again, finding her mouth. "You love when I remind you how well we still fit, don't you?"

She can't answer. She doesn't have to. He knows the truth; he feels it in the tension of her breath, in the relentless grip of her body, in the way she arches against him as though it's not enough, not nearly enough, even though it's already more than she thought she'd ever have again.

Another push. Another press. Another sound she can't quite suppress. His fingers work deeper, his breath hot against her temple, the way it always was when they couldn't get enough. She rides the edge of another shattering release, overwhelmed, ready, half-coherent and begging.

He doesn't stop.

She spreads her legs wider, arching against the relentless pace of his hand, the unyielding feel of him, barely able to hold herself together as he claims every inch of her, every breath, every silent, unguarded desire she didn't think she'd find words for.

"You want more?"

His voice is ragged, but his touch stays steady, stays hard. "Tell me, Claire. Tell me how much you need it."

It's not just her imagination this time. It's not just a silent plea that he doesn't know how to hear. It's real. It's what she wants. She finds his gaze and holds it, raw and open and exactly who she remembers.

"Everything," she whispers, but it sounds more like a prayer than a plea. More like a promise than a want. "I need—"

"Everything?" He holds her gaze, holds her body, holds nothing back.

He feels the shift before she says a word, knows what it means before it fully sinks in for either of them. Her wide eyes, her eager body, her submission to him and to herself and to the depth of her own goddamn want.

"—everything," she moans, barely believing this is real, barely holding on, barely hanging onto anything but the blissful pressure of his hand and the shameful, wonderful feeling of asking for all of it.

Then she lets go.

He pushes her further than she thought possible, makes her come so hard she forgets what it's like to pretend, makes her gasp and jerk and clench around his fingers as though she'll never stop shaking, never stop wanting, never stop craving what only he can give her.

Nate doesn't move at first. He just watches her. Watches the woman who used to disappear, now utterly undone beneath him.

"Don't think I'm done with you yet," he whispers, teasing, knowing, sending a second shock through her already spent body. "Not a chance."

He eases up, barely, then goes again. He doesn't give her room to breathe, doesn't give her a moment to overthink, doesn't let her get lost inside her own head or go anywhere else but here. His fingers keep moving, unrelenting, loving the desperate sounds coming from her mouth, loving the desperate wetness coming from her pussy, loving the way she bucks against him like she can't get enough, like she never wants it to end.

She should be exhausted. She is exhausted. But she's far too high on her own dizzy, weightless pleasure to even pretend she's tired. Her body is alive with sensation. Alive with him. Alive with need. And this time, she isn't afraid to ask. This time, she isn't afraid to tell.

She knows exactly what she wants. She knows he wants it, too.

"Oh god. Nate—" His name leaves her lips like a secret, like a command, like an open confession. "Fuck me. Do it. Take me."

Her legs tremble, but they don't close. They don't stop inviting him in. They don't stop spreading. She's completely unguarded, more exposed than she's ever been, and she doesn't know how much longer she can handle it. Doesn't know how much longer he's going to make her handle it.

Nate smirks, wild and tender and knowing, then lets the tension build until it's nearly unbearable. He knows the only thing keeping her together is the anticipation, the waiting, the torture.

He's wrong.

But only for now.

He trails his mouth down her inner thigh, teasing, breath hot and deliberate against her most sensitive places, dragging this out to the point of blissful cruelty. Her body jerks at the feel of it, her skin prickling with sweat and desperation. His mouth alone might finish her. Thinks she might come from the way he doesn't give in to her breathless urgency.

Not yet. He takes his time. Every second. Every sound. Every inch.

He makes her ride the edge again, but this time it's different. It's not the slow stretch of his fingers that has her sobbing for more. It's his lips, his teeth, his tongue, making her squirm and writhe and beg. Making her so wet, so sensitive, so overwhelmed, she can't hold on, can't hold back, can't believe she didn't fall apart the first time.

"Oh fuck," she gasps, feeling another climax start to take her, to unmake her, to spread through every quivering limb. "Oh fuck."

Her hips lift from the bed, but he keeps her pinned. He's as merciless with his touch as he is with the raw, hushed sounds she never thought she'd hear again. Sounds like: Don't stop shaking, don't stop letting go, don't stop, don't stop, don't stop. Sounds like: Nate.

She almost laughs from the blissful intensity of it. She almost cries. But she's too focused on his mouth, too dizzy from this new, unfiltered rush of wanting, too high on him and only him and goddamn him.

Another moan, another quiver, another messy, broken release, and he's still there.

She doesn't even realize she's panting his name until he pulls away. She doesn't even realize she's still shaking, still sensitive, still filled with that unbearable need, until she sees him grin.

She's too weak to move, too desperate to let go. He keeps her there, a wide hand between her legs, watching every breathless whimper and stuttering gasp, watching the long, vulnerable lines of her limbs as she grips the sheets and surrenders.

She doesn't flinch. She doesn't fight it. She doesn't look away.

She's still holding his cock, still holding on, still holding onto the belief that she'll find her way back to sanity when this is through. But she's not sure if she wants to be sane again. She's not sure if she wants anything except to be taken as deep and as hard and as unguarded as she can be.

And Nate knows.

He loves seeing her like this. He loves making her like this. He loves watching her strain and plead and clench around him, around his fingers, around his cock, even as she thinks she might shatter if she takes much more.

She thinks he'll finally give in, finally ease up, finally let her rest, let her recover, let her come down. But he's not done. Not by a long shot.

The buzz of the toy against her thigh makes her jolt. His grin tells her he's nowhere near done.

"Holy fuck," she moans, louder than she means to, louder than she's ever been, eyes wide, hips twitching as he brings it to the edge of her entrance. "Holy—"

He pushes it inside.

She's wet and shaking, lost to the rhythm, unable to tell where his hands end and her hunger begins. It's been a long time since they've done this. It's been too long. The soft hum of it blends with the sound of him, of them, the shocking fullness making her whimper and beg and press against him with a growing urgency she can't contain. She wants every last piece he promised, everything he whispered, everything they used to be before everything else took over. She wants all of it—his hands, his weight, his impossible knowing. She's already his. She always was.

Nate is greedy, but Claire is greedier.

The toy is enough to wreck her, enough to leave her exhausted and open and taken. But Nate doesn't stop at enough. He knows how she wants it, knows how she needs it, knows she'll let him do anything.

It's not just in his head. It's in the slick mess of her skin, the quick rise and fall of her chest, the wordless gasp as she gives in, gives up, gives him what he needs: her.

Every inch. Every breath. Every want.

"Is this too much for you?" he asks, a low rumble of playful, teasing, filthy reverence. "Can you even take this?"

She nods, barely coherent, barely able to process how deeply he's filling her. How much she loves it. How much he knows she loves it.

"Words, Claire." He holds still, impossibly, unbearably, as though the last hour didn't happen. As though she didn't already fall apart twice. As though he's just getting started. "Say it. Tell me."

"I love it," she gasps, no hesitation, no holding back, no one but him to hear the shameful thrill of being his good fucking girl. "I love it, Nate. I love it."

His pace sharpens. The slap of skin. The rasp of breath. Her sob tangled with his name—it's all she can hear. All she wants. He still has the control, but it's slipping, slipping, slipping with every buck of her hips and every clench of her legs and every desperate sound she makes.

"Jesus," he moans, louder, harder, unable to hold back. "You're going to make me come."

She needs that. She needs it more than he does.

"Inside me," she begs, but it sounds more like a challenge than a request. It sounds like a memory they both love. "I want it."

Then he gives it to her.

One final thrust, and she loses herself entirely. One final thrust, and she never wants to be found again. The toy falls from his hand, but he doesn't stop, doesn't stop fucking her until she can't breathe, can't think, can't remember anything except the way they fell asleep in the rocking chair, then in each other, then never again.

He's still there. Still inside her. Still watching like he can't believe how far they've come back to this.

# Four

Claire finds a stray crayon at the base of her wine glass, wedged between the island and her resolve. How long it's been there she can't guess. The new silence of the house unsettles her; each child miraculously occupied. One snacking. One coloring. One with his paci, halfway to dreaming. It's a flash of time that belongs only to her—unmapped territory, unpaved and unknown.

The stillness presses at her bones until the dryer buzzes, and she moves on instinct to the finished load, gathering warm clothes with shaking hands. She drifts toward the laundry room, hollow and untethered. This time, she remembers to lock the door.

Her heart kicks inside her chest, something urgent and alive, as if to remind her: yes. You are. She drops a handful of juice-stained onesies back into the laundry basket and lets the thought pulse beneath her skin. Alone, with the quietest house she's had in months. Alone, with no nap schedule or bedtime routine or bags of goldfish pressed into her palm. Alone, where the only touch is the one she gives herself. She leans against the dryer and lets the vibration hum through her bones.

She hadn't planned to lock the door. She hadn't planned any of it. The weight of a juice-sticky hand or a lukewarm bottle might come crashing through at any moment, reclaiming her. But not yet. Not yet. She grips the edge of the dryer, feeling the memory of last night thrumming back through her fingers. It was only a dream, wasn't it? The kind she woke from, aching and alone. The kind she only let herself believe when he was already gone for work, like it hadn't been years since his hands had been on her like that.

But they had been. Last night, they had been.

A sharp moan had pushed its way past her lips when his fingers ventured, filthy and familiar, to places they hadn't gone since before Heath. God, Heathie. All that time ago. Her mind races ahead, winding tight with the memory of Nate's filthy murmurs and a growled dare for her to be the one to ask for it next time. Plain. Unfiltered. Her fingers tremble and clutch at the dryer's edge as if the steel frame can keep her grounded. She lets the sensations travel through her—the vibration, the words, the empty ache. It leaves her gasping, off-balance and uncertain, like catching her reflection and finding herself changed in ways she hadn't agreed to.

Her hand moves to her waist. The yoga pants she's been wearing since Heath's pregnancy sag there, stained and soft as butter. Her fingers wander beneath the waistband, curious and unplanned. An inhale hitches in her throat as the pressure builds and her eyes press closed, clamped tight against the reality of what this moment means, and whose body it is that leans against the dryer. She bites down on her lip, tight, until it leaves an imprint. Until she feels full, on the verge, as if her body can't contain more than a soft click of the laundry room lock. A sound she can barely hear but fills her to bursting, deeper and more needed than her own hand. Deeper and more needed than—

The unplanned jolt of her release. It's been years since she's known this feeling: raw and beautiful and entirely hers. Her knees buckle. She drops, gasping, undone. Still more than just a caretaker, for now. For just a little while.

She didn't know she could still give herself this. That she was still hers to give.

Her phone buzzes from the laundry room counter.

Mom Club Confidential

Tues, Mar 5, 1:27 PM

Naomi

Did I leave a damn water bottle at your place again?

If it's pink and smells like chicken nuggets, it's mine.

Rachel

Changing the name of this chat before Claire gets us outed at school drop-off.

Rachel named the conversation "Don't Read This Aloud, Karen".

Naomi

Too late. I snorted coffee out my nose.

Claire

I'm dying. You're all going to hell with me.

✒

Claire breathes in the weight of it—air gone suddenly thin with the realization that she isn't alone. Her body shifts. Her eyes snap open. Her heart stretches toward the sound of Nate's approaching footsteps. They stop at the door.

Then the handle.

It's an impatient rattle, and she feels it all the way through. There is only one second, and then one voice. "Claire?" Her answer is silence. Her answer is waiting to see how far he will push this time. It comes as a second rattle, a pop, and a push into the room that takes her breath away.

Nate stands at the door, panting like the pursuit has winded him. It has. He never thought he'd find her like this—lost in her own touch, flushed, like she'd really followed through on his dare. The one he tossed out so recklessly when his fingers were already in deep. The one she'd bitten back a moan to answer, cheeks so bright, making him crazy. He never thought he'd find her so far ahead of him that he'd be left pounding at the door like an afterthought.

Her chest lifts and falls beneath the braless tank she's barely wearing, as if she's finding him new and different. Maybe she is. This version of him—the one who follows through, who doesn't leave her waiting—isn't the man she's known lately. Isn't the man who left every fantasy unfinished and unfulfilled. Not until last night. Her hands still shake from it, from the echoes and edges. From how deep they went and how easy it was, once they finally started, for him to pick up exactly where they'd left off.

Nate stares at her, all-consuming, as if he's already crossed the room and yanked the rest of her self-control out of her hands. As if the deep purple flush between her legs already belongs to him and they both know it. It leaves her breathless. It leaves her so hot with need she thinks she might die from it. He takes a single step toward her and pauses there, just one boot planted on the tile. A test, she knows, to see if she'll come to him this time. But she stays, she waits, she lets him do it all. Another few strides and he's across the room, dropping the laundry basket like it's everything else that stands between them. She doesn't move. She lets him take it. Lets him take her.

The push of his tongue against her bottom lip is filthy, shocking, deep. He groans, animal and raw, as his hips press her harder against the vibrating machine. It drives through her and she lets it, lets him, lets it all fill her so fully that her moan is the only thing left.

"Fuck," Nate growls against her mouth, tight and unplanned like her hand had been just moments ago.

Her head falls back. He's catching up. Finally. His beard grazes her neck and she shivers, a tiny clench that gets him exactly where she wants him. It can. It does. The shiver gets him pushing fast and unplanned and without even trying.

Everywhere. He is everywhere at once, greedy with the days and years and possibilities they've let slip away. She drowns in the frantic touch of his hands and the throaty catch of his breath. Every inch of her skin lights up under his palms. She melts into it. There is nothing but this and him and now and the wild electric tangle between her body and his, the deep, vibrating need she can finally give herself over to. The deep, vibrating man she can finally give herself over to.

The harder he goes, the deeper she gives in. He hoists her onto the dryer like there's nothing else in the world, and it only makes her burn for him more. Makes her even hotter to wrap herself around his waist and show him how far she'll let him take it. Her nails press into his shoulders as her knees spread wider, and he rips a deep, dirty moan from her throat.

Her back arches, her fingers twist, and she almost loses it.

Already.

Claire braces herself against the cabinets, soft white lines of pressure blooming under her knuckles, as Nate takes her with the same force that she's longed for and feared. He barely gives her time to register the feel of his body pinning her, the electric grip of his hands, before a deep thrust has her moaning into the hum of the dryer.

All of it fills her at once: the vibrations, the need, the man she still can't believe is finally hers. Her legs tighten, pulling him closer. His name slips from her mouth, a broken chant, until there's no space for even that.

She shakes with the want of him. Nate groans low and rough, feeling her already starting to lose it. The filthy heat of her breaks him, pushes him closer to the edge than he meant to be. Than he wants to be, because god, he needs this to last. Needs her to know how much of him there is, how fucking much he can give her if she'll only let him.

"Don't stop," she gasps into the airless space between them.

He wouldn't. Couldn't. Not when her legs have him trapped so deep he feels like he's inside more than just her body. Not when she's already shivering, caught between him and the hum of the dryer, already about to unravel around him. It makes him wild, makes him desperate, and he buries himself in her, fast and filthy and exactly the way she needs it. Her panties cut into the softness of her thighs, and her nails cut into the hardness of his shoulders. Neither of them lets up.

The sounds she makes say it all—high, raw, wrecked with relief. She's close, but she wants more. Needs more.

She bites down on her lip, hard, the same way she did last night when he made her the promise he's keeping now. Her back arches, tight, and her head tilts back, wild.

"Fuck, Claire," Nate groans as he fills her. She's almost as tight around him as the goddamn pants she's still wearing.

He lifts her higher, pressing her hard into the cabinets, like that's what she needs to really feel it. The angle makes her gasp and her body shudders, unhinged and overwhelmed. Her thighs start to slip from the wetness and her mind starts to slip from the wreck of it, but Nate won't let her. He grips her hips so hard she knows she'll bruise. She wants to. She wants to feel it, feel him, until it's the only thing left inside her. Until she's wrecked and reckless and as much of a mess as he can make her.

"Nate!" Her voice is a gasp, a cry, a wild and unhinged confession.

He loves it. Loves her, loves her like this.

She can't take any more and he won't stop giving it to her. The pressure and noise and everything builds until it's too much, until it's all of him and more of herself than she thought she could be.

Her nails dig deeper, her voice gets louder than the vibrating machine they're fucking on. She shatters around him, losing every thread of thought except how completely he owns her body.

Nate groans as he gives in, spilling into her with a raw surrender that leaves them both shaking. With heat and him. The room is small and airless and wild with noise, but Claire barely notices. Not when she's spinning so hard she can't see. Not when the whole world is reduced to Nate's low moan in her ear, the impossible squeeze of her legs around his waist, and the quicksilver explosion of more. More than she asked for. More than she can handle. More than she can contain, finally.

His chest heaves against hers. They stay tangled in sweat and cotton until breath returns, until reality settles, until they can believe this really happened. She gives him a smile, sated and bright, and it's the one thing he never thought he'd see on her again. Not like this.

Her knees go slack but his grip stays sure. There is nowhere for her to go. There is nowhere she'd rather be. She slumps against him, breathless and satisfied and laughing, and it is more of an answer than she's given him in years.

# Five

Claire fumbles with the cereal boxes, her fingers still thick with sleep, as the morning spills into their small kitchen. The children orbit around her in a blur of mismatched pajamas, limbs too long for the bodies they belong to. She half-hears their urgent demands for breakfast over the clatter of bowls and the first signs of bickering.

Nate is behind her, quiet as ever, loading the dishwasher with an efficiency that almost masks the undercurrent of tension. Yesterday's aftershock rattles between them, vibrating through the smallest actions—a brush of fingers, a shared glance, his palm resting on her hip a moment too long. It all says everything they're not, and as they move through the storm of morning routine, Claire wonders if this is how secrets start to bloom.

The routine should feel practiced, but every motion crackles with unfamiliar energy. Claire pours cereal into bowls, dodging her son's eager reach and her daughter's high-pitched insistence on the blue cup, not the green one. Milk sloshes over the rim, soaking into the cuff of her shirt, and she sighs as she grabs a dishtowel, tossing it to the floor to soak up the spill. Nate leans past her to grab a dirty pan from the counter, his chest brushing against her shoulder, close enough to make her breath hitch. He acts casual, easy, but she feels the pull of him as he steps back.

Claire rubs at a stubborn splatter of dried yogurt on the table, the cloth catching on sticky patches and crumbs, while the children's voices swell into a chorus of need. Nate continues to load the dishwasher, the clink of dishes punctuating the white noise of morning chaos. He's steady and calm in a way that soothes and excites all at once. She steals a glance at him, and he looks up just in time to catch her, his mouth quirking in that familiar, half-suppressed smile. It's not quite a secret, the way they're moving around each other. Not yet.

"Mom! He's looking at my cereal!"

"No I'm not!"

She tries to tune out their bickering, her focus flickering between the kids and Nate, between the mayhem and the memory of yesterday. They'd barely gotten their clothes back in order when the baby monitor crackled to life. Now she watches him unload more than silverware, his presence burning into the space they share. Another sideways brush, this time a deliberate grazing of fingers along her forearm as he reaches for a coffee cup. She shivers and shifts, pretending she needs to rearrange something at the counter.

Nate's nearness turns the whole morning electric. Claire feels it everywhere: in the lingering warmth where his skin meets hers, in the way her heart thuds when he passes behind her again, so close she swears she can taste him. She swipes a stray lock of hair from her face, leaving a streak of milk across her cheek. The intimacy is unexpected, a rope tying them together, dragging everything bright and alive through the blur of routine. He turns, the brush of denim and his palm connecting with her hip. A touch so simple it shouldn't matter, but it does.

Her pulse quickens as he rests there, holding her steady, and for a second, the noise of the house drops away. She knows he feels it too—the same thing she can't stop replaying in her mind, the sound of that lock clicking shut. His eyes flick to hers, searching, intense, before he pulls back with a measured slowness that makes her ache. She watches him, sees the focus in his movements, the care in the way he stacks plates and wipes countertops. Nate, her silent conspirator.

Breakfast is abandoned, then returned to, the table a sticky mess of cereal rings and spilled juice. Claire moves through the chaos with practiced ease, but beneath it, something pulls taut. It's in every fleeting look, every loaded pause. She sees the way he moves, purposeful and almost possessive, and she remembers the way he looked at her yesterday—like she'd slipped under his skin and stayed there.

By the time the first shoe is lost and then found, and the jackets are pulled on with the requisite whining, the whole morning feels like a promise wrapped in routine. Nate is already one foot out the door, but he's not really gone. She knows it in the way her body buzzes in the wake of him, knows it in the curve of his lips as he gives her one last glance. She's spent so many mornings on autopilot, numb to everything but the task at hand. But not today.

Today, everything hums with the tension of what's left unsaid, a secret as fragile and dangerous as the lock on that laundry room door. Claire pauses, letting the kids tumble out in front of her, and takes a deep breath. She doesn't know where it's leading them, but she knows she's not the only one wondering.

The house exhales into silence. The kids are asleep. Claire and Nate sit in the hollow space between them, waiting. She folds towels, cotton soft beneath her fingers, trying to keep busy. Nate sits close enough for her to sense his unspoken intention, but far enough to make her wonder if she's imagined it.

The hum of the dishwasher echoes their quiet tension, a background noise to the conversations they're not having. Claire resists the urge to fill the silence, to pin it down with questions she's afraid to ask, but then Nate's voice cuts through, low and casual: "So... that thing yesterday. In the laundry room." It's not a question, and yet it asks everything.

Claire's breath catches, and she hesitates over a corner of towel, the pause so long she thinks she might forget how to breathe. The words hang in the air, each one a tiny universe of possibility and risk. "Yeah?" she finally responds, forcing her voice to sound normal when everything about her feels anything but. She doesn't look up, her eyes trained on the task in her lap, as if neat folds could organize her chaotic thoughts.

She hears him shift on the couch, his body making soft, denim sounds against the fabric. It's such a small thing, but it sends a jolt through her, the space between them suddenly immense and fragile. "I liked it," he says, and the simplicity of the words hits her like a physical force. She swallows hard, gripping the towel a little too tightly, feeling its fibers press into her palm.

"Me too," Claire manages, the words tasting like relief and longing all at once. The admission is out, simple and enormous, and she lets herself meet his gaze for a heartbeat that stretches into eternity. His eyes are on her, intent and unguarded, and she feels herself softening under their weight.

The silence reclaims the room, dense with everything they might dare to want. Claire turns her attention back to the towels, pretending they require her full focus, but her mind is spinning through the past twenty-four hours. The way he'd unlocked the door this morning, the way her body had sparked to life at the sight of him. Was it a fluke, a one-time slip back into who they used to be? Or had they turned a corner so sharp there was no going back? She doesn't realize she's holding her breath until Nate speaks again.

"Should we," he starts, voice casual but serious, "I don't know... make that a thing?" He shifts his gaze, as if suddenly fascinated by the grooves in the hardwood floor, and Claire feels a wild urge to laugh or cry. A thing. As if it could be that simple.

She forces herself to sound calm, in control, when she's anything but. "A thing?" she echoes, still pretending to focus on the task at hand. Her heart hammers, wild and uncontained, betraying her in its rhythm.

She can sense him choosing his words, feel the tension stretching between them as he pauses.

"Like... a rule." The quiet intention of his voice makes her shiver. "If the door's locked..." He doesn't finish the sentence, but he doesn't need to. The implication unfurls around them, bright and dangerous. Her pulse races as the full weight of it lands in the space between them.

Claire forces her hands to move, folding a towel with deliberate, precise slowness. The effort to stay composed is almost enough to break her. She looks up, locking eyes with him, letting the shared tension become a kind of daring. "Then it's on," she says, giving the words a weight that is anything but casual.

The silence that follows is different—charged, like the air before a storm. Nate nods, a single, decisive motion, and a hint of that crooked smile edges onto his lips. Claire feels a rush of something wild and exhilarating, a pulse of hope that beats beneath the uncertainty.

The dishwasher hums on, steady and relentless, as they sit together in the warm cocoon of unspoken promises. Claire lets herself imagine the door locked again, the freedom in those small, contained moments. Her heart swells with the thought that maybe, just maybe, they can have this. Her mind spins forward, imagining every future click of the lock, every unspoken declaration it might bring.

Nate is still halfway in his truck, the engine a low, reluctant growl beneath him, when he decides. He's supposed to make one more stop, pick up a part or a tool or some other piece of their orderly, patched-together life, but instead he's home. He takes the long way, letting his mind play through the morning in tight, breathless loops, his foot tapping the gas pedal with impatient hope.

And when he pulls into the drive, body already quickening with the thrill of yesterday's remembered promise, he hears it: the solid click of the laundry room lock, snaking through the distance, direct as a phone line. Claire's calling him. He doesn't hesitate.

The familiar clang of metal on metal fills the truck as Nate cuts the engine and steps out. The sound reverberates, urgency thrumming in his bones. He crosses the short distance to the door in quick, purposeful strides, setting his tools down in the mudroom without pausing. The bag hits the floor, an afterthought. Nothing else matters but the tight, exciting pull of what he's about to find on the other side.

The lock is a beacon, calling him with the clarity of Claire's voice. The house is quiet, conspiratorial in its stillness. Nate stands at the edge of their silent understanding, the world narrowed to this door and what waits behind it. His hand hovers over the handle, feeling the heat of intention before he makes contact.

This morning spins through his mind in quick, vivid flashes—the kids yelling over cereal, Claire's sidelong glances, the thrill of every touch. He's been playing it back all day, his focus shot and body on a constant, maddening edge. When he'd decided to skip his last stop, it was with a hope so reckless he hardly dared admit it. But now, with the lock clicking into place as his feet hit the porch, it feels like a new kind of certainty.

His hand grips the knob, and he tests it with the lightest pressure. Locked. Exactly as they'd planned. A new wave of adrenaline crashes through him, swift and bright, and he fumbles only slightly as he reaches into his pocket for the small tool he'd brought inside yesterday. The metal is cool and sure between his fingers, the act of unlocking it so familiar, but now charged with everything they've dared to set in motion.

Inside, Claire stands with her back against the washer, breath coming fast and eager, each exhale a release of everything that's coiled inside her. She hears Nate's truck door slam shut, hears his footsteps echo through the garage, and then the handle jiggling as he tries it, careful at first, testing their shared secret. Her heart leaps at the resistance, at the proof that she's called and he's answered. The wait is a sweet kind of agony, each second a tighter knot of expectation.

Her body tingles, every nerve a live wire, as she imagines him on the other side of the door, finding the lock in place and knowing she's here, waiting. Waiting to be found, to be taken, to be his. Her pulse is a quick, insistent drumbeat as she hears him work the lock, the seconds stretching long and dizzy before she finally senses him getting it right.

The door swings open, slow as a confession, and Nate fills the doorway, a silhouette of intent and promise. Their eyes meet across the small space, the air vibrating between them like the hum of high tension wires. They are quiet, still, holding the moment in breathless suspension. His presence hits her, warm and immediate, and Claire shivers under its weight.

Then he's in the room, closing the door with one swift, decisive motion that shuts the world out. She feels the tremor of the lock sliding back into place, hears its soft, final click, and it undoes her. Her body moves before her mind can catch up, and she's in his arms, a collision of relief and want and oh my god, you're here.

Nate's hands are everywhere—fisting in her hair, pulling her hips flush against his, slipping beneath her shirt to feel the heat of her skin. It's a greedy, glorious tangle, and Claire gasps as his mouth finds the curve of her neck, teeth grazing the tender spot that makes her knees go weak. She's electric, buzzing with him and the secret they share.

"Nate," she breathes, the word half-plea, half-wonder, as his fingers find the edge of her leggings and push them down, down. He's quick, deft, working her bare with a single-mindedness that sends a fresh wave of desire pooling low in her belly. He tugs her shirt over her head, taking the bralette with it, and she's standing naked before him, exposed and trembling, but so sure in the way he looks at her.

He stops, eyes dark and intent, and lets the heat of his gaze travel the length of her. "Fuck, Claire," he groans, his voice rough and reverent. "You have no idea..." He doesn't finish, can't finish, because his mouth is on her again, hard and hungry, and the rest of the world drops away.

His jeans are off, a quick, eager motion that leaves him stripped and ready. He wraps one arm around her waist, pulling her tight against him, the sensation of skin on skin so overwhelming she thinks she might come undone before they even start. "You wanted this," he murmurs, the words a velvet growl in her ear.

She nods, a sharp, desperate movement, fingers digging into the hard muscle of his back. "Yes," she gasps, and it's everything. Permission, confession, plea. "Please, yes."

He lifts her, hands firm on her ass, and she wraps her legs around his hips, the position so perfect it steals her breath. She can feel how much he wants her, hard and ready against her thigh, and her head spins with the wild, dizzy relief of it. Nate carries her to the counter, setting her down with a controlled force that makes her moan.

She reaches for him, for his cock, needing the hot, solid proof that this is real. He stops her, takes her wrists in one large hand and holds them over her head, using the other to dip low between her legs, finding her wet and wanting. Claire lets out a sound that's almost a sob, arching into his touch, her whole body a conduit of need.

"You're killing me," he mutters, voice low. "I've missed *this*. Missed you like this." "You're killing me." He pushes two fingers inside, and she gasps, her whole body pitching forward, chasing the rhythm he sets. She watches him, the way his mouth curves in fierce satisfaction, and it sends her spiraling. She's right there, already so close, and it's almost too much.

"Nate," she cries out, his name a shattering of consonants, vowels, everything that holds her together. "Please, I'm—" But the rest is lost, a choked moan that turns to whimpers as he withdraws his hand, leaving her empty and desperate.

He lets go of her wrists, and she almost collapses into him, every nerve straining for more. "I've got you," he promises, voice so steady and sure she wants to wrap herself in it. He flips open the lid of the toy box, retrieves a bottle of lube, and coats his cock in quick, efficient strokes that make her whimper. "I've got you."

Nate positions himself at her entrance, and Claire thinks she might die from wanting. She digs her nails into his shoulders, wordlessly urging him to take, take, take, and when he finally pushes into her, slow and controlled, her vision whites out.

"Fuck, yes," she gasps, clenching around him, every muscle taut with the exquisite, overwhelming fullness. It's too much and not enough, a sweet, unbearable tension that has her head falling back, hitting the wall with a soft, dull thud. Nate holds her there, watches the way she unravels for him, and it's everything.

He rocks into her, measured and relentless, a rhythm that builds and builds until Claire is teetering on the edge, broken sounds spilling from her lips with each thrust. "Look at me," he orders, voice tight and commanding, and it pulls her back from the brink, focusing the storm inside her.

She meets his eyes, and the intensity there unspools her completely. He's taking her, yes, but she's taking him too, the act so consuming and mutual that she doesn't know where she ends and he begins. It's new and familiar, messy and precise, and when she comes, she takes him with her, the last of her control shattered in a cry that echoes off the walls.

He follows her over the edge, holding her hips as if anchoring them both, the deep, guttural sounds he's making setting off another wave of pleasure that grips her tight. They stay there, bodies locked and trembling, until the aftershocks subside and the air around them stills.

They collapse against each other, a tangle of limbs and breath and sweat-slicked skin. Nate brushes damp hair from her forehead, kisses the spot with aching tenderness, and Claire feels the lock settle back into place, a promise as solid and real as the man holding her.

As their breathing slows, she nuzzles into the curve of his neck, and a satisfied, drowsy smile tugs at her lips. Claire smiles against his skin. "We're really doing this."

Nate's breath huffs against her hair. "Yeah, we are."

The lock clicks back into place behind them.

# Six

It feels like they're doing this just to mess with her, she thinks. Or to have something to hold over her head when she shows up to wine night two minutes late with the excuse that "the kids were a lot tonight" and not nearly as creative as Naomi's last one, which involved her three-year-old gluing his hand to the backseat of her luxury SUV.

Claire catches the cloud of notifications on her lock screen one last time before they buzz away like a gnat

Every message is unhinged. Every woman is over it.

And Claire? She's already halfway out the door, keys in hand, mascara on point, heart finally in it.

Mom Club Confidential

Wed, Mar 6 at 7:32 PM

Naomi

bring wine. don't care if it's 8.99

Naomi

and don't bring kids.

Harper

god I hope someone says "discharge"

Rachel

Evan can go fuck himself

Brielle

i'm wearing pants with a zipper tonight so NO ONE FUCK THIS UP FOR ME

Brielle

DELETE THIS

Claire checks the time. If she waits any longer, they'll think she's running late because she was actually doing laundry and not… other things. Like refilling her glass and whispering just a little more, a little deeper, oh my god, don't stop before heading out the door.

✒

In Naomi's house, there's not a single plastic train or chicken nugget in sight. It's clean and calm and Pinterest-perfect, exactly the kind of place Claire imagines when she thinks of a pre-child version of herself who could finish a thought, a project, or a sentence without needing to refill anyone's milk cup.

It's a universe away from her own cluttered house, and she's half convinced Naomi uses them all as test subjects for her impossibly orchestrated dinner parties: look at these poor exhausted souls! Imagine what I could do for you!

The front door opens before Claire can knock, revealing Naomi's latest feat of carefully planned hosting: a full spread of alcohol, snacks, and Instagram-ready friendship, complete with coordinated charcuterie board. There's no telling what Naomi has planned, only that it's probably labeled in a secret Google Doc with contingencies for wardrobe malfunctions, unexpected toddlers, and getting cut off at wine number three.

Somewhere between a hip-looking houseplant and an overpriced throw pillow, Brielle declares, "Is it fucked up that I don't know how to sit in jeans anymore?" She kicks off her shoes and plants herself on the couch, her toned legs crossed in a way that makes Claire simultaneously jealous and grateful that Bri is the one person who doesn't care that she showed up in a t-shirt she slept in.

Rachel rolls her eyes but pulls out her phone. "If no one says 'discharge' tonight," she mutters, thumbs working with machine-like efficiency as she captures a perfect shot of Naomi's wine selection, "I will personally make a toast." Her glossy black bob doesn't have a single hair out of place, and she's wearing a posh new "fuck me" dress that would put Sex and the City-era Carrie Bradshaw to shame.

Harper is the next to arrive, in all black with a sharp tongue and sharper eyeliner. Claire never knows if she should laugh or cringe when Harper opens her mouth. She likes that about her. "We need to establish some rules here," Harper deadpans. "Like if you say the word toddler more than twice, you have to chug."

Rachel raises her hand and winks. "I'm fine with this."

They aren't the kind of friends Claire imagined herself having—not with Rachel's perfectly curated life, or Naomi's strict adherence to color-coding, or Harper's cold but brilliant humor, or Bri's refusal to commit to anyone or anything—but they've quickly become the people who keep her sane when she can't hear her own thoughts, the ones who look at her sideways and tease her until she finally bursts.

Naomi has the kind of closet that Claire might actually murder for, and even when they're being casual, she looks like an Athleta catalog. Claire immediately knows the outfit Naomi opens the door in: it's the kind of outfit she used to plan, coordinated without being obvious. Soft cardigan, lace peeking underneath, perfect curls that look effortless but Claire knows actually took ten minutes in a mirror and some kind of styling tool she has never bothered to learn the name of.

"Someone take a picture," Naomi sighs, posing with an artfully placed hand on the side of her face and the side of her hip. "This will never happen again."

Claire used to be the planner, the creative, the girl who coordinated her own outfits and her own events before Rachel dubbed them the "Mom Club" and they all stopped pretending to be put-together. Now she just throws on something clean enough to pass for an actual wardrobe. Which, at the moment, happens to be a second-hand top from Rachel, a pair of shorts, and a shrug of wine-fueled confidence. She doesn't care that the color is two seasons ago. It's not going to be on her for long.

"Claire!" Brielle's bright voice fills the space when Claire finally makes it through the door. "You look… like you need a drink." She pats the empty cushion beside her, shaking her head at Claire's thrift-store look.

Harper smirks as she fills Claire's glass and passes it across the room. "Is this one of Rachel's?" she asks, fingering the sleeve as Claire collapses on the couch. "We have to burn it."

The burn doesn't land; it vanishes into an alcohol-laced giggle as Claire's tired body hits the cushion. Brielle snaps another picture, and within seconds everyone's phones buzz with the latest update. "Day drinking?" Bri asks, staring at her screen as Rachel chokes back laughter and nearly a mouthful of wine. "Or is there something we don't know about you?"

Rachel leans in close, scrutinizing Claire's expression, and nudges her side. "Did you get a sitter? Your face looks very we're-not-doing-laundry-tonight." She leans back, eyes narrowed, and adds, "Someone's husband is getting some."

The observation sends Claire into another fit of laughter that she can't stop, a kind of laughter she didn't even know she had in her a few weeks ago. She used to think she didn't need this kind of night; she used to think the cracks in her marriage would just close up, or that she'd be fine if they didn't. The journal she kept was a reminder, an escape, a fantasy that gave her back the pieces of herself she was sure were gone for good.

But then the pact started.

And it's why she's here, why she feels alive enough to keep laughing until everyone's staring and the wine nearly spills from Brielle's phone to Claire's shorts.

It's why she doesn't know what to say when Bri asks if there's something they don't know about her. Because there is, but she doesn't know how to tell them without admitting she kept her wild, sexy secret under wraps for a year.

The night unfolds with the same chaotic rhythm of their group chat, but with more alcohol and less chance of anyone having to stop mid-sentence to prevent their child from playing with an open flame or joining the party. The rooms of Naomi's picture-perfect house echo with laughter and half-drunk confessions and Claire's coy avoidance of any real answers.

No one mentions toddler more than twice; no one has to chug. They have two solid hours of freedom as partners and grandparents take over parenting duties, and Claire can't remember the last time she felt this loose.

"This one time?" Brielle starts, loud enough that the words echo over the sharp angles of Naomi's vaulted ceiling, "Julian and I tried to—" She cuts herself off, her laugh turning infectious as she motions at her phone. "Yeah, actually, no. You don't get this story."

Harper stares, deadpan. "Is that what it's like when you're off the clock? 'Yeah, actually, no'? Real hardcore there."

Rachel nearly spits out her drink and nudges Claire with her elbow. "How do we say this?" she teases, a perfectly manicured finger resting on her chin. "Our little Clairebear has been acting... differently." She waggles her brows and leans back against the crisp, color-coordinated couch. "What do we think is going on here, ladies?"

"We're not doing laundry tonight," Naomi mimics, tossing her hair over her shoulder in a practiced motion that belongs in a shampoo commercial.

Brielle snaps another photo with her camera, while Harper catches it with her words. "Okay, Claire. Spill. You've been glowing for, like, a week."

It's more like three weeks, Claire thinks as the words blur and vibrate in her head.

Three weeks since Nate closed the door and asked, "This what you wanted?" in a voice that didn't expect a yes, because her phone was full of unread fantasies and her eyes were tired and he thought he knew the answer until he didn't. Until she said, "Yes, fuck, don't stop, don't stop, don't stop," like a different version of herself.

It's more like three weeks since Nate locked the laundry room door with a quick, practiced motion and slid his hands into her shorts with the same confident ease. She remembers the feel of his fingers—how different it was than the way she imagined—rough, deliberate, getting her wetter with each slow stroke until she forgot how exhausted she'd been an hour earlier. It's more like three weeks since he reached for the toy she thought he didn't know about, coaxed her against the vibrating dryer, and filled her with both his thick length and the quiet, unspoken promise of another night like this one.

✒

Claire wants to tell them, but all that comes out is a glassy, embarrassed, I've been keeping this under wraps for a year and don't know how to say it kind of laugh. She wants to tell them how things shifted, how her dream—the one that broke the numbness between Nate and her, the one she had to write down so she wouldn't forget, the one where she didn't care who saw or who heard—became real.

But she keeps the words in for now, watches her friends pass knowing looks, and feels the intoxicating buzz of all the other things that haven't stayed in: toys, fingers, a hard length, the plug that made her squirm and scream and hold onto Nate like he was the only thing keeping her on this planet when he stretched her so tight and so fucking full.

She takes a deep breath and holds it as long as she can before she gives in to another wave of laughter, louder than before.

Her friends don't believe her deflection of "I'm just sleeping better" for a second. They've never seen her like this; they know she's hiding something, that she's bursting. And so is Claire. She doesn't care if it comes out as a laugh, a gasp, or a quick breathless cry when she opens the door later and Nate is there, and he's all hers again.

✒

A game called "Fantasy or Fiction" lights up the room as soon as Rachel mentions the word cock ring; wine sloshes into glasses with each loud guess, and flushed faces turn to Claire when she whispers the question that gets Naomi refilling her drink and Harper asking, "Is that what we're calling it now?"

Naomi crosses her legs and stares Claire down. "It's not real until you say it," she taunts, dark red hair pulled back into a severe but chic bun. "Now tell us what's going on with you."

It's easier to keep the words in when she isn't drunk and surrounded by the best group of prying wives anyone could ask for. "You all sound like horny teenagers," Claire deflects, picking at the hem of the hand-me-down shirt that's starting to grow on her. She takes another sip, and another, while Brielle declares, "One hundred percent real. I've probably read it," and Claire knows she's not just guessing.

Rachel flips to the next index card, and the stack looks suspiciously well researched. "We do sound like horny teenagers," she admits. "I like it. Next one! He's a trauma surgeon. She's a brat who won't follow the rules." She looks up, eyes sparkling, her voice all bright, tipsy amusement. "Or is that too close to home?"

✒

Naomi raises her hand, three fingers outstretched like a girl scout pledge. "Real. And I bet it's rated three stars because it didn't count unless she tied him up and put it in his ass."

Rachel holds up her glass. "To discharge!"

"Jesus, Rachel." Claire's laughter bubbles up again, louder and more spontaneous than before. She almost lets out the words, almost tells them, almost spills every delicious detail she swore she wouldn't until Brielle saves her.

"Way more than three stars," Bri counters, cutting into Naomi's toast. "Trust me. I'll loan it to you." She's all smiles, the playful ease of her voice almost like music. "Or did someone here write it?"

This time, Claire's the one holding up her glass. It's nice not to be the one with the most embarrassing secrets.

✒

They're off the clock. They're loud and loose, and they keep bringing up cock rings, which sends Claire's mind spinning with both fantasy and memory. In another life, she wouldn't have been embarrassed to write about that kind of thing. She's kept the impulse buried for so long that she almost forgot about it—almost convinced herself that fantasies are easier to keep when they aren't shared.

It doesn't help that Rachel's dirty "fiction" sounds a lot like the ones Claire can't stop imagining, the ones Nate has somehow made more than fiction these past few weeks. He's not a security guard, not a trauma surgeon, not a hot cop with a gun to match, but it's hard not to think about him like that when she's buzzed enough to let her mind wander to places she never thought it would again.

He's not the kind of guy who does these things, the Claire she used to be thought. It would feel weird to ask. What if it's awkward? What if it makes him stop wanting? She knows better now. But it took time, and nights like this one, and moments like when he got rougher with her than she imagined and she begged, shaking, fuck, Nate, more, more, oh god, don't stop.

Claire stays quiet, but she's not as quiet as last week, and the week before, and all the weeks before that. The room buzzes around her, a flurry of alcohol and secrets that taste like the wine she wasn't bold enough to bring until now. She bites her lip, her grin like a tightly wound spring.

"What happened to 'just sleeping better'?" Naomi teases.

Harper side-eyes her. "Come on. Don't make me ask twice."

"Come on," Rachel cuts in. "Something changed."

"I did." Claire gives them the vaguest of shrugs and the boldest look she can muster. She remembers when they used to be her lifeline, her last-ditch attempt to find herself again, her escape. She doesn't need escape anymore, but she needs their energy, their friendship, their fuck-it-all attitude. She doesn't want them to stop asking, even if it takes all night to get to the truth.

"I think this is the last bottle," Naomi sighs, refilling glasses with cheap red before settling back into her own. "Better than getting pregnant again."

Harper nods. "Or being awake at 2am."

"Or admitting Evan is too tired to fuck me."

Bri gives Rachel an incredulous look. "You're shitting me."

"Nope."

"Well that sucks."

"Seriously."

Claire watches her friends break into couples, a flurry of quick stories and quicker glances and the same kind of barely suppressed tension that she felt before the pact, before the dream, before Nate pushed her further than she thought she'd go. It won't be long, she thinks, before someone else in this group takes her lead.

Naomi corners Rachel on the floor, while Brielle takes Harper on the couch.

"What are the odds?" Bri asks.

"Higher than you'd think," Harper snaps back.

And the teasing goes on and on, until Naomi is flat on her back with a pillow behind her head, Rachel straddles the end of the couch, and Brielle flips Harper off with a smirk.

✒

"Two years." Bri rolls her eyes and takes a long sip, then holds up a finger. "Wait. No. A year. He got his new office chair right around the time we—"

Harper squints, her eyebrows arched in disbelief. "A chair? Are you saying his ergonomic back support is hotter than you?"

"I'm saying Leo's going to wish he was this chair."

Claire stares at the couch, where Rachel is leaning back against the cushion, lips pursed. "Micah's contract," Rachel says, blowing her bangs off her forehead and clinking Naomi's glass, "isn't the only thing his boss is riding him on."

Naomi puts a dramatic hand over her chest, mock-scandalized and way too amused. "You think I can't handle that information?"

Rachel shrugs and grins. "I think you need another drink."

"Okay, but only if you tell me about this fucking chair. He'll never see it coming."

Claire holds her glass tight and tries to catch every word, every secret, every hint that their relationships are a bigger mess than she thought.

It reminds her how lost she felt before the night Nate closed the door, touched her in ways she had to dream about, and proved that the husband she wanted—the husband she wrote about—was closer than she thought.

✒

"Now it's my turn," Rachel cuts in, stealing Claire's attention before her mind goes any further from the room. "Are we done with the last bottle yet? Are we?"

Naomi barely finishes her drink before Rachel starts again. "She's a mom of three. He's a cowboy with a pair of handcuffs and a tight pair of jeans." She scans the room for a reaction, but this time it's not Claire who gives it to her.

Naomi nearly chokes. "Sounds familiar?" She laughs and lets the words hang over the room like an old joke. Claire used to hate when they teased her, but it feels different now, lighter, less like a punch in the gut and more like a punchline she's happy to run with.

"Someone might be," Claire counters, an eye-roll in her voice and a buzz on her lips. "Are we really out?"

Rachel pours the last drop of the last bottle and nods. "Yes. But I feel a liquor store run coming on. Some of us are just starting to remember."

The wine's almost gone, and so is the tightness Claire used to carry with her to these kinds of nights.

Just a couple weeks ago you were… Naomi starts, but Claire cuts in, unable to stop the smile on her face from reaching the rest of her. "Sleeping? Tired? Not screaming?"

Harper lets the word hang in the air as she holds the door for Rachel.

"Come on," she calls over her shoulder, not one for drawn-out goodbyes. "Someone here has definitely done it in a laundry room."

The last of the wine buzzes in Claire's body like the texts that came earlier: fast, insistent, impossible to ignore.

"Not everyone," Brielle says as she trails Naomi out the door. "Just the lucky ones."

Their voices fade down the driveway, leaving Claire alone with a light head and a tingling that only gets worse as she thinks of how far away her laundry room is.

It's not just the wine that's doing it; it's not just her friends' laughter and not-very-subtle attempts to pry a confession out of her. It's how quick and wild her mind goes when she thinks about everything she couldn't say out loud. Not just how much Nate surprised her when he got rough and dirty, not just the hard length of him pushing inside her in places she didn't know she'd love, but how much she surprised herself when she begged for more.

Nate wouldn't know what to do with a cock ring, she used to think. And I wouldn't know what to do with a fantasy.

Now, she knows. Now, it doesn't take much to feel breathless, giddy, as if the hint of a cowboy in handcuffs could push her over the edge before she makes it halfway home.

It doesn't take much to know exactly where her night is going, or who's going to remember this version of her best.

The leftover wine pulses in Claire's veins, syncs with the pace of her racing heart, while a charged memory vibrates through her body with the same urgency as her footsteps from Naomi's door. The night winds down, but her breathless anticipation only grows.

Rachel's laughter echoes as she half-fumbles, half-flies toward her car: She's a mom of three. He's a cowboy with a pair of handcuffs and a tight pair of jeans. Claire had laughed too, carefree and loud, letting the wine and the jokes buzz in her body like a swarm of impatient messages: don't care if it's 8.99. Sleeping better? More like better than all of us.

She was breathless. She still is. The heat in her cheeks flares as she thinks of Nate, how he pushed her against the washer, how every slow thrust sent a jolt through her, how he didn't hold back when she begged for more. The sensation was so raw, so all-consuming, she couldn't breathe, couldn't speak. When they finished, he cupped her face and waited for the world to come back, steady, quiet, filled with promise. He always waits, and it drives her fucking crazy in the best possible way.

This time she doesn't want to wait.

She fumbles with the keys, half-drunkenly and a little out of breath. The porch light is on, like he's waiting for her, like he's listening to her heart pound and her head spin and her body scream. She thinks of the dream again—how fast and rough he took her, how much she wanted him to—and she pushes her front door open in the kind of hurry that gets even Claire surprised at how bold she's become.

Inside the quiet of her own house, she pauses to catch her breath. It doesn't take long; the pause only makes the need worse.

She's surrounded by toys and clutter and reminders of the wild, messy life that sometimes feels too big and too close and too much to hold together. She feels different now, unsteady in a way she loves, like she's breaking all over again but in the best possible way.

Her own house is nothing like Naomi's. There's not a coordinated throw pillow in sight, and that's okay. It's not pristine, not manicured, but it's hers. Warm, imperfect, alive. There's an energy that Claire didn't notice before she poured herself a glass of wine earlier, before she slipped into the bedroom for what was supposed to be a quick drink and turned into the best possible start to a long, needy night.

It feels like Nate, she thinks. Like them. Like things aren't just drifting anymore.

She knows they'll keep this going; they'll keep finding ways to fit the real them into the rest of their chaotic lives. That was the promise, and it felt big, like the promise of not drifting through everything. Like not being ghosts. Like seeing, feeling, touching.

Her heart pounds and her core tightens with a different kind of heat when she remembers how Nate touched her before she left, slow and hard and with his fingers deep inside. It was only supposed to be a taste, a reminder, a preview, but he couldn't stop and neither could she. Her hurried goodbye turned into a frantic, all-consuming, I can't wait.

He told her to think of it when the others asked what's different. Now, it's all she can think about.

✒

A low buzz pulls her attention to the counter, where her phone vibrates with the last volley of group texts. The screen is blurry and her head is fuzzy but she can still read their words, breathless and laughing:

Oh my god, someone really
did it. Laundry room.

Her cheeks flare again, hotter than the wine and brighter than the giddy blush of being caught with the hints she didn't want to hide.

When she started hanging out with the others, the best Claire could do was an awkward grin and an occasional flustered response. Her face used to match her words, subdued, quiet, like the edges of a life that was all fine, fine, everything is fine.

Now, she types with bold fingers and flushed cheeks, less worried about saying the right thing, more worried about the wait until she gets to feel this breathless again. She doesn't hit delete when she taps a new message:

Claire

...Some of us are just
starting to remember.

They can say what they want. Claire has more to say. More to do. More to hold onto.

✒

She lingers in the entryway, but not for long. She knows where this is going. She knows how this ends. She knows how this feels, and how good it is, and how much better it will be in five minutes. It's all too much to handle and all too hard to let go. It's a fast and slow burn at the same time, and Claire can't stop drifting toward it.

There's a sudden but welcome impatience in everything she does; she can't get through the house fast enough, can't relive the memory of Nate pushing her against the dryer enough. The anticipation is so thick it almost leaves a trace in the air, the same way the kids leave smudged fingerprints on the sliding door when they get so restless they can't wait to get outside.

But this isn't like that. It's waiting to get in, not out, to see and feel, to burn and hold.

She doesn't even stop for her shoes, which she kicked off on her way out and left where she thought she might be too tired for a round two by the time she got back. She knows she's going to crash hard when she makes it to the bedroom, and she wants to crash as fast as she can.

A sharp pulse runs through her as she stands in front of the door and sees a sudden flash of what this will be. She leans her head against the cool wood and tries to savor the feeling of not knowing, of being breathless, of hiding the real her and finally letting the real her out.

When she does push the door open, she's flushed, shaking, buzzing.

The anticipation she felt in the hallway only gets worse when she sees Nate stretched out, waiting, like nothing has changed. But everything has, and she feels like she might burst the way she did earlier, except it's a different kind of burst, a messier one, and one she can't laugh through the way she did when Naomi pushed a glass into her hand and teased her until she was dizzy.

"Long night?" Nate's voice is soft, low, but not quite as soft as the look he gives her. She bites her lip, knowing she has no chance at holding in her words or her breath when he gets his hands on her again.

She pushes the door closed, remembering how he pressed her hard against the wall. How he filled her. How he wrecked her in the best way. When he entered her from behind. When she was stretched so tight she could barely speak or breathe. When they came together in the quickest, hottest, loudest moment they've ever had.

She wants that again, and he knows it.

She wants that again, and it drives her toward him.

Her bare feet barely touch the floor as she drifts through the space between them, fast and deliberate, like her heart. She doesn't have to rush, she tells herself, but she wants to. She doesn't have to drift, but it's okay if she does.

She doesn't have to do anything but feel, like this, like everything.

She lets the door swing shut.

She doesn't want to wait.

✒

In the dim, private space of their bedroom, Nate traces the length of Claire's damp skin with quiet intensity, closing the gap between want and touch. Their kisses deepen, their bodies collide, and the last two hours feel like the longest of her life as she writhes under his demanding hands and unfaltering thrusts.

She's breathing too hard, too fast. She's feeling too much, too soon. Her skin burns under his hands, and her shorts are already on the floor before she has a chance to answer him, to say anything but his name. He moves her like it's the only thing that matters, so steady, so sure, that she can't keep up with her breath, her words, her body.

"Better than 8.99?" he murmurs, breathless himself as he guides her to the bed.

He knows it was; he knows it is. He sees the way her pulse races. He feels the way she stretches against him like a taut wire, about to snap.

The heat of his body is everywhere—surrounding her, pushing against her, taking over every inch of space and skin and air. The soft cotton of his shirt, the rough callouses of his hands, the familiar length of his body; everything sends her into a frenzy. Everything makes her feel like she's finally unraveling, losing the threads she kept wound tight when she laughed and flushed and tried not to touch herself while the others guessed.

It's not guessing now. She knows exactly what's going to happen, and it feels fucking amazing.

His fingers curl around the hem of her shirt, moving up, up, brushing her bare skin until the fabric and the air between them are gone. Her need is insistent, greedy, and she's never been happier to feel like it might never be filled.

The world falls away in a mess of tangled sheets, tangled limbs, tangled breaths. Claire arches her back, presses herself into him, loving the frenzied, desperate rhythm of his hands and lips and unrelenting touch. She's going to come apart, and she's going to love it, and she's not going to hold back, not when she's this wet, this full, this stretched.

His fingers slide inside her, thick and wanting, and she's gone.

She writhes and squirms, and it's not like before—when she thought it was gone, when she thought he was too. Her cries are louder now, breathier, full of shock and satisfaction and longing. She's lost, clutching him, thrashing against him, wondering how the fuck he's still holding on. Every push and pull leaves her trembling, arching, begging, oh god Nate, don't stop, don't stop.

His body is strong, unrelenting, hard against hers. He grips her waist, brings her close, shifts her so he's above her, around her, everywhere.

His fingers press in deep, curling just right, dragging a gasp from her as her hips grind into his hand. His pace is brutal, greedy, and she gives him everything. Slick heat spreads between her thighs, loud and filthy as he fucks into it without mercy. She braces herself, but he takes her deeper, harder, rough enough to leave her aching tomorrow. Exactly how she wants it.

It's more than she imagined. It's more than her body can take. It's more than anything but him.

"Fuck," a sharp cry rips from her lips, "fuck, yes, yes—"

The plug slips in deep, and her cries catch in her throat. He stays steady, waiting for her to beg, testing the tight limits of her body. She doesn't know how long she can last, how long she can hold it in.

He knows she's not the only one.

"Want it?" he asks, knowing she does.

Claire gives him her body, her breath, her voice, but it's not enough. She wants to give him everything.

She loses track of her cries, her breath, herself. His hands hold her still, his thrusts make her wild, and the entire room spins with an intensity she can't keep up with. She can't remember the last time she wanted like this, the last time she had like this, the last time they went for a round two and she wasn't holding back.

Her memory spins and fades and fuck, she doesn't want to remember. She wants to feel. She wants to feel it like this forever.

The past weeks crash together, a blur of tight, filthy, late night everything. Her friends' laughter and Nate's steady promise tangle and unravel until it's all she can do not to scream.

"Don't stop, don't stop—"

He moves his lips down her stomach, slow, hard, wet. She grips the sheets, digs her nails into the mattress, not sure how much longer she can keep her hands off him.

But she loves it, she loves him, she loves how he fills her with each steady, deliberate, agonizing stroke of his tongue.

Her thighs clamp around his head as she writhes beneath his mouth, words lost to the frantic, guttural sounds clawing up her throat as he pushes her right to the edge. He holds her thighs, spreads her wider, gives her more, faster, until she forgets everything but his mouth and her desperate, breathless pleas.

She wants, and he gives.

He watches, and she comes undone.

She feels it, all of it, as it should be: Nate, his lips, his tongue, his thick fingers working her as she arches and moans and swears she'll never stop.

✒

The more she gives him, the less she can hold back. His mouth moves in a punishing rhythm, his fingers curl inside her, his body shifts to replace what she loses. He moves with her, against her, all around her, and it drives her to the breaking point.

She gasps, shudders, so fucking close, and Nate thrusts hard, pulls her legs over his shoulders and buries himself inside. His fingers reach for her clit, and his cock pushes deep, like the last three weeks condensed into a single moment of raw, forceful intensity.

He knows exactly what to do, and so does she.

Her release catches fire. Her cry rings out. Her whole body comes in a wave of ecstasy and disbelief as she feels him push and fill and fuck her to the core.

She's still clawing for more, and he's not about to stop giving it.

Claire wraps herself around him, pulls him deeper, wanting every inch of him, wanting more than she thought possible. His rhythm is steady, hard, and just this side of reckless as they climb together, as they beg and scream and make up for the lost, numb, drifting months when she thought she couldn't want like this again.

Nate flips her on top of him and she rides, unrestrained, wild, gasping for more, faster, yes, please, more. Her body tightens and she forgets her words, just wants to take him, feel him, fuck him in every way.

She doesn't have to do this; she wants to. She doesn't have to be loud; she loves to. She doesn't have to be the version of herself she thought she lost; she knows now that she never lost it.

Her nails rake his chest, his teeth graze her lip, and they're caught in a rough, wanton pace that burns, screams, does exactly what Claire fantasized.

They've gotten loud these past few weeks. She loves it. He loves it. His hands press hard against her waist, against her back, against her messy hair. He pushes deeper, hips grinding until she's pinned wide open, stretched so far she's dizzy from it.

He hauls her onto her knees, palms bruising her hips as he drives in deep enough to make her vision blur. Her body quivers and clenches and she doesn't know how she's kept it in, how he's held on, but it's all coming out. Every inch of her, every part of him.

She thought they lost this, but she was wrong. They've just begun.

Claire gasps, holds, feels. She's pinned wide open, gasping into the sheets, dizzy from how deep he's fucking her. The friction is maddening. He drags her up, bends her over, shoves in deep. No slow build, no pulling back. Just raw, filthy possession until she's choking on moans and clawing the sheets. His cock hits deep and cruel, and she takes it. Loves every fucking second of it.

The room shakes with each wild, messy cry. The neighbors might hear; she hopes they do. Her hands grip the headboard and she moans, pleads, explodes, more than she's ever let herself. Nate gives it back, drives it home, lets her be the loud, dirty, unrestrained version of herself she almost forgot.

He holds her like this, not slowing down, even when she thinks she might lose it, even when she screams, when she comes, when she begs. She doesn't know how they're still going, how they're still loud and filthy and fast. It's so much, too much, He's deep inside her, every thrust stretching her wider, dragging filthy sounds from her lips. It's everything she thought she'd forgotten how to want.

His possessive thrusts drive her mad. It's the hottest thing she can imagine, the loudest thing she can say. She knows it's coming, and she doesn't hold back. Neither does he.

It happens all at once and it's the best thing ever, fucking ever, forever.

They're flushed, breathless, completely spent, but he can't stop. He pushes hard, pushes through, keeps it going. He fucks her deep, keeps her there, his grip and his cock and his voice anchoring her to every filthy second of it.

She collapses, they both do. It's reckless and tender and hotter than anything she thought they'd have again. It's everything she needed, everything she thought she lost. Her heart pounds. Her skin burns. She can't stop, won't stop, until they crash, breathless, wild, hers.

They stay locked together, not wanting to leave this moment, not letting each other go. He never wants to stop, and Claire never wants him to. Her pulse is fast and so is his.

When it slows, when they fall asleep in a tangled, tight mess, she still feels it. The promise. The edge. The heart-pounding relief of not losing him. Of being lost in him.

✒

Her body aches but she doesn't care. Her heart pounds but she's too far gone. She wanted this, and it's everything, everything, more.

They stay locked together, sweaty, exhausted, wrecked in the best way. Not letting each other go. Not wanting to.

When sleep finally claims them, Claire knows this:

They're not done. Not even close.

# Seven

Claire has too many piles.

Pajamas folded like soft paper cranes, perched on the dresser, on the bed, on the floor, ready to be redistributed, resettled. Pajamas with robots, stripes, little bears climbing into the knees.

And Claire—one empty nest—right there in the middle, squatting on her heels, squinting at sizes.

Will these even fit him next week?

Will she remember where they go?

Her breath clouds the air like mid-winter, not one damp degree below summer. Rain presses at the window like a child's nose.

The bedroom feels enormous.

So does she.

There's a flash of movement and a squeak in the hallway—tiny, retreating footsteps—and she's alone again.

Until she isn't.

He comes to her without words, holding everything Claire didn't know she was missing in his calloused hands.

A small black box with a three-number code.

He places it on the nightstand, reverent, like an offering. Then Nate walks into the bathroom, shutting the door, leaving her to the clutter of pajamas and possibilities.

Her heart climbs wild in her chest. She knows exactly what's in the box.

She stays there, stunned, waiting for him to reappear as if she's waiting for a revelation, but she can't stop staring at the box. It's long and narrow with a silver trim and hinges like an antique. Old-fashioned and elegant, but when she holds it, it hums like an engine. She almost doesn't want to open it, doesn't want to risk that familiar flood of longing, but she wants to be ready when he comes back, ready when he finally looks at her with the heat she remembers. Her fingers trace its edges. She doesn't even try to unlatch it.

Weeks ago, Claire never would have imagined this. She had come back from the Mom Club's latest "workshop" laughing about all the sex toy reviews that had descended into group texts and chaos. An hour later, Nate cornered her in the kitchen with a hesitant smile, asking her quiet, loaded questions about trying new things, about anything she'd be open to. She couldn't find words to answer him, just a hard nod as he pressed her up against the fridge. They didn't make it to the bedroom that night. Didn't make it to the bed since. Now, her stomach flips at the reminder that he hasn't forgotten.

She sets the box down, gentle, and feels its weight in her chest. There's that flash of motion in the hallway again—a blur of purple and yellow pajama tops, a wailing cry, a sudden crash—and then there's Nate, standing right in front of her. The only sound is the faint patter of rain against glass and their ragged breathing.

Claire hasn't moved a muscle.

His worn jeans hang low on his hips, feet bare, hair mussed and damp like he's just stepped from the shower—or wrestled toddlers into bed. Or both. When she looks at him, really looks, he's the only thing in the room.

The only thing she can see, the only thing she wants. He doesn't touch her. He doesn't have to. He knows her that well.

Nate stands beside the bed and pulls the covers back, the fabric a soft rustle that's somehow loud in the otherwise silent room. Claire watches, breathless, as he makes a space for her. Her own heart makes it impossible to hear anything else. He doesn't say a word, just waits. He knows her better than she does. That's what terrifies her. That's what she wants most.

The tension coils inside her, something like hunger but deeper. Claire sits on the edge of the bed, finally unclenching her fingers. Her limbs are molten, unsteady, but when she slides toward the space he's made, when she lies back and sees him there, everything loosens, blooms.

She doesn't recognize the woman looking up at him, lips parted, breaths shallow, needy. She never thought she'd see her again. She can't believe she's already back.

She wants to ask him a hundred things. How? Why? Where did he get it? Does he think she's ready for this? But the only question that matters—do you still want me—he's already answered. His sure, solid presence is the only response she needs. When Nate moves, when he reaches for the black box, she thinks her body might break apart with want.

He flicks the latch open with the ease of a secret he's been waiting to tell. The box opens. So does Claire.

Nate draws it out with long fingers, handles it like it's precious. A little jewel-toned plug, slim and elegant and silk-soft to the touch. He watches her closely, the roughness in his voice low and reverent when he finally speaks. "I can stop. Say no. Say anything."

She knows he means it. He'll stop if she asks, if she needs a moment, a night, a year, if she can't remember how to be who he wants anymore. His words fall into the wide space of the room, into the wide spaces between them. Claire doesn't say no. She doesn't say anything at all.

Nate watches her for hesitation, but all Claire feels is reckless need. Her skin burns everywhere his fingers land. Her breath hitches as he parts her thighs, leaves her open. The soft grey pants he loves—worn to hell, already soaked—cling to her skin. When his gaze catches hers, she's too far gone to blush. All she can do is lift her hips and beg without words.

She could tell him: Take me. Fuck me. Make me forget. But his hand slides beneath her waistband, knuckles grazing skin, and she knows he already hears it. Her gasp becomes a moan as he moves lower, discovering slick heat with slow fingers. She's so wet she can hear him smile in the low rumble of his voice: "That's my girl." A simple phrase, but it tears right through her. Her breath catches as he teases her open, drawing circles that make her legs tremble. Every sound she makes is an invitation, please and more and yes.

Nate is watchful, deliberate, letting her come undone before pushing his advantage. Claire hears herself whimper when his hand moves, when he grips her waistband and pulls, leaving her bare and needy. He could have her like this, right now, but that's not what he's planning. She watches him retrieve the box, the one they keep hidden, the one she used to dream about opening. Its lock gives way with a click, and she forgets how to breathe.

Nate takes his time, finding what he needs. When he's back between her legs, she's writhing, desperate to be touched. She doesn't even recognize her own voice, so thick with need. "Please," she whispers. It's a confession. An admission. And it gets her exactly what she wants. The small pink toy is terrifying only because she wants it. He makes her watch as he coats it in lube, slick glistening on his fingers. He kisses her stomach, still avoiding her most sensitive spots, letting her anticipate, letting her want. He slides a pillow beneath her hips, and her muscles tense. The position leaves her exposed, desperate. The low, controlled hum of his voice floods her system as he warms the plug between his hands, telling her how beautiful she is, how fucking sexy.

He presses it against her, careful and coaxing. Claire gasps at the unfamiliar sensation, intense and urgent. It doesn't hurt, but it's so much. So full. Her body resists and gives, stretches and clings, pleasure and pressure twisting together until she can't tell which is which. Her legs quake with the effort of adjusting, of taking him. She digs her heels into the mattress, grounding herself against the intrusion. "Good girl," he says. Those two small words are her undoing. She's lost and found all at once, shuddering as she opens for him. Her pussy is soaked, more than ready for what she knows is next.

Pleasure sparks through every nerve, sharp and electric. She surrenders to it, gives herself up to the sensation of being taken. Her moans turn wild as her body takes him, the slick glide overwhelming and perfect. Her husband groans, guttural and raw, but doesn't let the pace falter. She's doing this for him. For her. For them. Taking it everywhere. A rush of want spikes through her, sudden and savage, when she thinks of how they must look right now. Nate deep inside her, the toy shifting with each thrust, her legs barely able to hold on. She doesn't care that it's almost too much. She doesn't want it to stop.

The steady rhythm is her undoing. She's trapped beneath his weight, stretched open, every motion intense and shocking. The plug shifts again and again, fucking her with the force of Nate's cock. Claire shakes, feeling everything, reduced to gasps and sobs and 'please please please.' She doesn't recognize her own voice or her own need. He pulls her closer, thrusting deep, and her whole body convulses. Then he stills, making her feel the stretch, the grip, the impossibility of it all. It's savage and perfect, possession with no escape.

Orgasm explodes through her, fierce and unrelenting. It leaves her raw, trembling, obliterated. He thrusts again, and again, until she's shattering around him. Her skin tingles with it, nerves on fire, every part of her swept away. It's devastating and relentless, each new wave wrecking her more than the last. She doesn't even know what she's saying, just a jumble of Nate's name and needy cries. She's lost to it, forgetting her own identity, forgetting the world outside this room.

She can't catch her breath, not with him still moving. His pace is brutal in its control, measured and steady, pulling new sounds from her throat. He doesn't let up, not for a second, not even as she thrashes beneath him. Not until she has nothing left, her body weak and spent. Only then does he come, spilling deep and hot inside her. Claire's vision blurs as she drifts, hazy and complete. She feels him there, everywhere, so impossibly full. Everything she wants. Everything she never knew she could take.

✒

Claire opens her eyes to find Nate looking at her like she's a miracle. A revelation. Everything he needs. It's the same way she feels. Her voice is still lost, her body still limp, but he hears her anyway. He draws her in, holding her close, anchoring her with the solid warmth of his chest. The sensation is too big for words. So is what it means. So is what it will become.

Her cheek rests against his skin, breath soft, fingers brushing the faded t-shirt that clings to his ribs. They tremble there, exhausted and alive, not quite sure what to hold onto. They don't have to. He cradles her anyway, so secure, so firm, the way he hasn't in what feels like years. The wild pulse of him matches her own, and Claire is swept up in something even bigger than what just wrecked her. More terrifying. More amazing. More. Her heart surges with the realization that it wasn't just sex. It was the beginning of everything she thought she'd lost.

She breathes in his scent, laundry soap and desire and them. The thud of his heartbeat surrounds her, impossibly steady. Impossibly hers. She never wants to leave this spot. She never wants to leave him again. They're knotted together, limbs tangled, two halves of a whole she can't believe they almost lost. He watches her like she's new. Like he's new. Like they're both exactly what the other wants and needs. Claire's stillness becomes its own form of reaching out, of saying things she doesn't have words for yet.

His hands find her hair, loose from its braid, draping across her flushed skin. She feels so completely his and herself at the same time. Safe and daring. Secure and surrendered. All of the things she almost forgot she could be. Claire presses closer, knowing he understands. Knowing that after this, after him, after everything, she can never go back to the version of herself who didn't believe he still wanted her.

Her breath slows. Her heart doesn't. It swells with every second he holds her. With each second she lets him. She thinks of how far they've come in just a few short weeks. In one intense, overwhelming, fucking perfect night. She lets her mind drift, hazy and content, to how far they'll go. The laundry room was just the start. A door she thought was closed forever is opening, and Claire is brave enough now to step through it.

Her muscles ache, but it's a beautiful kind of exhaustion. It's the first time she hasn't felt a pang of guilt for feeling so good. Her mouth still can't find his name, but her body does. The way she molds against him, skin to skin, chest to chest, is its own kind of confession. Her own kind of worship. Nate doesn't let go, not for a second. Not even when she shudders against him, the aftershocks of the best orgasm of her life still humming through her system. He kisses her temple, and Claire wonders how she ever thought this part of their marriage was over.

His grip is loose but constant, a promise to be right there when she catches her breath, a promise to take it away again when she's ready. He doesn't ask if she is. He doesn't need to. She lifts her chin and presses her lips to his throat, a simple gesture, but it shakes him as much as his praise did for her. She can tell. She knows him. She loves him.

She sinks into the strength of his arms, how warm, how solid, how present he is. Claire hasn't let herself want anything this much in so long. Herself. Nate. The impossible combination of both. She nestles against him, feeling fragile and strong and everything in between. She lets herself believe. In them. In him. In this.

The silence doesn't fill the room—it cradles it. Like her. Like him. Like everything they didn't lose. Louder than her cries, his groans, the shared sounds of falling apart. Claire's breath evens out, and Nate tightens his hold. The act is its own kind of shattering. They stay like this, anchored together, absorbing the intensity, basking in what it means, where it will take them. The trust of it all. The possibility. The tender, exposed, soul-shaking beginning.

# Eight

Claire waits in front of the mirror, her skin flushed and her hair a mess around her shoulders.

It's late—the kitchen quiet, the house dark—but she stands there, daring herself to stay. She's a coward with this, usually, shying from her own reflection. Tonight, though, something's shifting. She wants to know what Nate sees when she forgets to hide. Her skin looks soft, like it belongs to someone unburdened. She takes a shaky breath and imagines him behind her, lifting her tank top with rough hands and words that burn. She is terrified and aching, strung between the urge to dress herself and the one to strip.

She tugs at her tank top, pretending it's not on purpose, pretending she doesn't want this more than anything. Her reflection is daunting, a reminder of everything she pretends not to need. A different kind of mother could pick up and go to bed, but she's bare-legged, chest heaving, and waiting for her husband to walk in and find her like this. Claire lets her eyes travel down, past the swell of her breasts and the sliver of her stomach. She doesn't feel like the woman in the glass—unsure and longing. Her hands are trembling when she pushes the hem up a little higher, teasing herself with the stretch of cotton against skin.

The last time he touched her like this, she couldn't look. Didn't have the nerve to meet his eyes, to see herself the way he does: lost and hungry, flushed and falling apart. She closes her eyes and remembers his hands. Rough. Greedy. Pulling her back to him as the plug slipped inside, making her gasp and moan and shake. Claire opens her eyes again, braver now. She wants to see. Needs to. What he does to her, what it feels like to give in and be ruined by it.

A deep breath, then another. She can almost feel his hands, real as ghosts, urging her to stay. This time, she tells herself. Just once. This is what she's wanted since he pushed that first boundary, since he made her watch herself start to crave it. Claire pulls her hair to one side, lets it tumble over her shoulder. Her heart is beating too fast and she's already wet, already nervous she'll lose her nerve. She stands, waits, lets the silence wrap around her. She can hear the hum of the dishwasher, the tick of a clock, the pounding of her pulse. The house feels dark, too big, empty. Her arms circle around her waist, and she wants to keep waiting but doesn't know how long before the moment breaks her.

The door clicks open, just slightly. A breath of time, a pause that hangs like a sigh. She sees Nate's reflection before she sees him—one shape, then two, then there. He stands in the doorway, a shadow at first, the dark outline of someone watching her. Her skin prickles, and a low, raw excitement flares. This is where she should look away, but she doesn't. Can't. Instead, she straightens. Lets him see. The truth of her, the part she hides. Her panties are pink, her breasts almost visible under the white tank, and he's still watching, as if she's something new. Her chest aches as he steps closer. He doesn't look away, and this, Claire knows, is the part that will undo her.

Nate moves like a man who's wanted this longer than he's willing to admit. Like a man just as scared. Claire trembles, her legs unsure but her heart knowing. He's coming to finish what he started. The thought makes her head spin, full of dirty words and things she can't say out loud. Her eyes are wide when he reaches her. A ghost of a smile tugs at his lips. It does her in.

"Stay here," he says, rough already. She thinks she might come apart just hearing it.

He stands behind her, close enough that she feels his breath at the back of her neck. She's already damp and throbbing, her body begging for more than his gaze. Her hands twitch at her sides, dying to touch him. Or maybe just to touch.

"Look at you," Nate murmurs, eyes fierce in the mirror. "You begged without a word. You think I didn't hear it?"

She watches his hands come up and settle on her waist. Heat floods her cheeks, but she doesn't look away. It's a small victory. A step closer to unguarded.

He moves slowly, deliberately, making a moment out of every inch. Claire's stomach flutters as his fingers slide up, tugging the hem of her shirt higher. Her breath hitches when his thumbs brush beneath her breasts, a promise of things to come. She wants to close her eyes but forces herself not to, makes herself see it all: how soft her skin is, how his hands look on her.

Nate leans down and kisses her shoulder, hot and open. Claire shivers and tilts her head, giving him more. Letting herself take more, too. His stubble scratches her neck in that way that's rough enough to remember, tender enough to miss. Her shirt creeps higher, her pulse echoing every move. This is what it feels like to come undone. This is what he does to her. This is what she wants.

Her breath turns shallow, her body melting under his touch. He peels the shirt over her head and tosses it aside—impatient, free. The air chills her bare breasts, but his hands warm her again, full and firm. Claire's lips part as she leans into it, as he cups and lifts.

She looks fragile, like something that could shatter. Her eyes dart from her reflection to Nate's, as if to ask if he's seeing this too, this woman so new and breakable. She lets out a little whimper when he pinches her nipple. She's always been quiet in bed, but that's starting to change. He watches every flicker of pleasure in her face, silent and intent. Her cheeks are pink and her skin feverish.

"That's it," he tells her, voice darker now. "Just like that." Claire's legs go weak at his praise, at his low, filthy certainty. Her body knows what he wants, even when she doesn't. Even when she's not sure if it's okay to be this exposed.

A gasp escapes her lips, and Claire has never felt more bare, more out of control. Her thoughts jumble as his fingers dig into her hips, guiding her back. Her legs tremble as she presses closer to him, needing to feel all of it: the stretch of her want, the burn of his touch.

The tension builds in her belly, sharp and real. This is happening. The mirror feels too honest, too big. But she can't look away, not even as she starts to. Not even as her body gives in and begins to fall apart.

✒

Nate's already on his knees behind her—a worshipful supplicant, making Claire his whole world. Her tank top is gone. His touch is a thousand places at once: hips, thighs, bare skin he's never let himself love like this.

She's unsteady but doesn't fall. Maybe that's why he does this to her—why he looks so hungry as he peels her panties down her legs, as he murmurs for her to watch. Claire is too undone to deny him, her body flushed and aching, full of raw edges that need his hands. When he rises to kiss her neck, she arches like she's the prayer.

Her legs are shaking. She's trying to breathe but can only manage a small, wrecked gasp as Nate slides the panties to her ankles. It's too much. It's not enough. Claire grips his shoulder to steady herself, to make him see how hard she's falling and how fast. He moves slowly, deliberately, like a man unraveling a secret. Like he can't quite believe she's letting him have this.

Nate's eyes are dark, more of a promise than she's ready to take. She shivers, thinking of all the ways he might keep it. "Don't look away," he tells her. Claire's heart jumps at the certainty in his voice. A command. A threat. A gift. She doesn't want to look away, but it scares her that he knows. That he's not afraid to push her that far, and farther.

He's not afraid of anything, she thinks. Not like her, flushed and trembling in front of the glass. Her reflection is too honest. Fevered, flushed, already needy before he's really begun. Her pulse hammers in her throat. She wants to close her eyes—but doesn't dare. Not when he sees this much. Not when she might miss it.

She should be ashamed. The thought barely registers, wiped out by the urgency of Nate's hands. He leaves her panties where they fall and rises to kiss her neck, making her arch back and melt into him. His lips trail over her jaw and down to her collarbone, open and possessive. His body is solid behind hers, grounding her in this instant, in this knowing. Claire whimpers, a fragile and helpless sound, not recognizing her own voice. Not recognizing her own face as she watches.

She doesn't recognize herself in the way her knees buckle when his fingers slip between her legs. Two, knuckle-deep and claiming, sliding inside without a pause. Her legs spread wider, like an offering she doesn't remember making. Her lips part. Her head falls back. His thumb circles her clit, building the need she already feels. Claire can barely breathe, barely stand.

"Fuck," she gasps, unable to hold back or pretend. Not this time. Maybe not ever again.

"You love this." Nate's voice is low, urgent. His fingers work her harder, pushing her further, her wetness glistening as he moves. "Say it."

Claire almost loses it from those two words alone. She opens her eyes, dazed, and sees herself spread and reckless. Her cheeks burn at the sight, the truth. At knowing he's watching her become someone else.

"Say it," he tells her again, relentless. "I want to hear it."

"I love it," she admits, her own voice raw and strange. More desperate than she knew. More like the woman in her dreams. Her heart thuds against her ribs, and she can't stop. "I love it. I love you."

Nate groans, a sound so filthy and satisfied it sends shockwaves through her body. He presses deeper, rougher, making her arch into him and whimper. Her eyes go wide as his other hand grips her ass, as a finger slides toward that forbidden place.

Claire's world goes blank when he touches her there. The rest of her goes slick and wanting. He circles her in a way that tells her he knows exactly what he's doing, in a way that reminds her of how she came apart the first time. The time he was less sure. The time she begged and then tried to hide.

"Watch," he whispers, eyes dark and knowing. "Don't look away."

She holds on to him, to the last shred of composure. Her fingers dig into his forearm as he takes her further. As she lets him. Her skin burns with the twin intensity of his touch. His hands drive her wild, coaxing her deeper into the frantic stretch and slide of his fingers. Claire's knees give but Nate holds her up, his strength a comfort she clings to.

She's never wanted anything this much. Not the way she wants him to keep going. Not the way she wants to see how far this can take her. Claire's body shakes as the pleasure builds, relentless and overwhelming. As he pushes and she gives, over and over.

"Look at yourself," Nate says, the strain in his voice telling her he's as far gone as she is. "Look how wet you are. Look how fucking beautiful you are."

His words make her dizzy, unsteady. So real she can't think. Claire trembles, knowing she's not going to survive this. Knowing she's not supposed to. She's shaking too hard to pretend she doesn't love it, love him. She lets out a wild, unguarded sound, desperate and real.

"Watch yourself fall apart," he tells her, raw and honest and hers. His fingers work her with more urgency, not stopping. Not when she's this close. "Watch it."

It's too much. She wants more. The truth and the giving. The wild, wrecked girl she's never been, not this free. Not this bare. Her body knows what it needs, even if she doesn't. Even if it's too much to hold on to. She is frantic now, pulsing around him. Right there. Almost gone. She watches the moment Nate said would come, the one that leaves her breathless. She sees herself lose everything.

When the climax hits, it rips through her. Intense and raw and absolute. Claire cries out, shaking against him, not holding back. She falls apart, just like he said, her legs giving and her thoughts shattering. Her skin flushed, her pulse unsteady. His fingers are wet and perfect and hers.

And she watches it all, just like he told her to.

✒

Claire collapses into Nate's arms, ragdoll-limp, shaking but complete. He's solid against her back, holding her together, holding her close. She grips his hands, as much an anchor as a plea, and never wants to let go. She's barely breathing, chest heaving with aftershocks and relief, the reality of what they've done.

Nate kisses her hair, her neck, every part of her he can reach, and she shivers at his touch. At the softness she can let herself feel now. "That's what I see," he tells her, like he's been holding it in. "Every time." Claire's eyes flutter closed, and she nods, sinking deeper, understanding. Her skin is flushed but her heart is safe. This time, it's safe.

Her breath is ragged, slowing as she comes down. As she comes back to him. Claire feels Nate's grip tighten around her shoulders, his need to keep her from slipping away again. She leans into it, lets herself have it, the one thing she hasn't known how to take in years.

Her skin is warm, and his chest feels strong against her spine, a steady comfort she wants to wrap around herself and hold.

She's shaky but more secure than she's been since before the kids, since before everything changed. Her eyes stay closed, too raw to see, but the darkness feels sweet now, full of promises that won't break. She never knew the truth of herself like this, never let herself find it. And Nate was there all along, ready to show her, ready to give her more than she'd let him say.

He kisses the side of her mouth, gentle and wanting. Like a first kiss, not a last. "Every time," he tells her again, a whisper more honest than she deserves. Claire nods, clings. She can't manage more than that, not yet, not while she's still floating. She's free-falling but held so tight. Nate holds her tighter, whispering, and his breath on her skin feels like more than just air. More than just love.

She sinks deeper into him, lets herself believe it's okay to do that now. The trembling slows. Her lips part with the softest sigh, and she's still open, still wanting. Her heartbeat is loud, but the urgency of before fades, a slow, beautiful aftermath. It feels endless and wrecked, a new and thrilling place.

"Claire," Nate says, his voice rough and tender. She hears his need and how it mixes with his relief, with hers. He sounds more raw than ever, more hers. He sounds like he's not going anywhere, not when she's still learning how to breathe. "I'm here."

That's enough to bring her back, all the way back. She's raw, exposed, and totally, completely taken. She didn't know it would be like this. Didn't know she could want to stay so much. Claire feels a small, dazed laugh rise in her chest, wild with the truth of everything they just did, everything that's still waiting. It bubbles up, soft and shaky, and Nate's arms close tighter. She has it, all of it. She thought it would scare her more. She thought she would still be scared, even now.

Her skin is damp, flushed, her hair a mess around her cheeks. She's more alive than she thought, more whole than she knew. The ragged beats of her heart start to find their rhythm, and Claire feels something shift, like it's just the beginning of a new, unfurling now. A beginning that pulls her toward him, that lets her hold on. She grips Nate's hands, not hiding anymore.

The world outside is dark and waiting, but she doesn't let go. She doesn't want to. This is where she stays, pressed into him, and it's enough. More than. This is what it feels like to be known, to be unafraid. This is what she needs, and she didn't even have to ask.

The quiet stretches around them, both a comfort and a reckoning. It doesn't feel empty now. It feels full and waiting, ready for the rest of it. The after, the parts where she sees herself the way he does, the way he always has. The raw openness that scared her before is softer now, not so much a weakness as a promise. She's beginning to believe him, to know he means every breath. She's beginning to believe herself.

When Nate speaks again, it's barely a whisper. Barely a sound at all. "I've got you," he murmurs. It feels like an echo in her chest, a perfect echo.

"Don't let go," Claire says, a plea and a sigh, unsure which one it is. She stays curled against him, not ready to move, not when she's starting to see. The moment stretches, long and real and beautifully small. She closes her eyes and sinks into it, sinking deeper than she thought she could.

When she sleeps, it's more of a dream than any dream. A floating softness, an unbroken mirror. She's watching again, but it's different this time. She's unafraid of the girl who looks back at her. Nate stands behind her, but she's the one who feels tall. She's the one with steady hands, reaching for the reflection. When she wakes up, she knows it will still be there.

It will still be enough.

# NINE

Claire moves like something new now, hips swinging, chin tilted, as if she's only just learned what those parts are for. Nate sees it first when he walks in and finds her barefoot in the kitchen, less mom and more mistress. There's a glow in her cheeks—the first blush he's seen in years that isn't from exhaustion or the kids.

Her eyes fix on him with a heat that doesn't flicker or fade. There's no turning back. No changing her mind. He hooks his pinky around hers. Claire doesn't let go—not until they're breathless in the bedroom, trying to forget they're married.

Her body is her own, as unborrowed and unsurrendered as it's been in years. She moves through the house with a new and curious confidence, almost reckless with it. She's light on her feet, silent. Sensual, she hopes, with an easiness that makes her laugh and drop laundry baskets and ignore calls. No self-consciousness, only motion. Only want. As if every part of her is stretching into something new. Even her old top-knot is losing its hold, loosening into a wilder shape as she speeds around.

Lately, everything is messier in this different way: the way it was in the beginning.

Crumbs always seem to dust the kitchen floor. Toddlers unearth toys, bits of dirt and playground sand, sticky surprises in each pocket. But none of it clings to her or slows her down, as if their grip is loosening and there's air between it all. Lightness. As if she can float above it, finally, like she's wanted to do since it first became overwhelming. Nothing pulls her down; nothing pins her in place.

Especially not with him on the way.

When Nate walks in, a slight sunburn kisses his neck, the only clue he's been working outside. His brown hair is a little sweaty and deliciously shaggy. That tired look of his, so rugged, meets hers in the soft late-afternoon light. What once felt like two houses on separate lots now fills the same room—electric, dizzy with possibility Nate's expression changes as soon as he sees her. As if he can sense the heat she feels pulsing everywhere, a flood rushing to her cheeks and the tips of her fingers and the spaces between her toes.

It's a look he hasn't given her in so long.

A look like he's seeing her. Just her, only her.

Their eyes lock, a crackling silence swelling between them like a whisper and a secret and a dare.

Claire smiles, biting her lip to keep from bursting, from saying yes or please or now. They don't need to speak. She doesn't need to ask. He can read every inch of her as easily as he could back when they first began, when they used to leave bars early and end up in rooms as anonymous and anonymous as the nights themselves. When he looks at her now, she's never felt more known.

He steps over something of the kids' on his way to her—two something's, three—but Claire doesn't even notice or care. There's no guilt for what she knows she's abandoning, what she knows they both want too much to feel any shame in. It feels different to be this hungry and this free at the same time.

In a single, wordless motion, Nate's pinky curls around hers. That small touch—deceptive and innocent and very much not—is enough to take her breath and start her moving. They leave the crumbs and mess behind, their long hallway narrowing and fading until it disappears.

He pulls her into the bedroom, almost like he's a kid again, like they both are, getting away with something they shouldn't and getting more and more reckless the farther they go. They stumble to the bed, out of breath from the steps they've taken, from the desire not to turn back or remember their own names.

Familiar anticipation surges through her—alive, urgent, like a knot in her chest tightening until she can't tell if it's ache or pleasure. It feels like every night of not knowing that becomes knowing again. Every glance that becomes touch that becomes yes.

Nate guides her to the bed, but they never make it that far, not yet. Not until they pause, catching each other's breaths, waiting for the space to change like it always does. From shared, silent, suburban: paint chips from the walls. Two lights, two nightstands. Tired, secondhand, polite.

Into something that is only them.

This time is not like any of the times before. Nate takes control of their quiet bedroom, not needing the cramped laundry room or other tight, guilty spaces. Not needing to hide what they are doing, even from themselves. This time, they do not want to finish quickly or wait to be discovered. They only want to begin.

They start when Nate unhooks his pinky from hers, reaching for something across the bed—just out of sight. He doesn't look away, even for a second. Not when he grabs the towel. Not when he opens the top drawer, that single move setting Claire on fire, so hot and alive she doesn't know where she will go to escape it or if she wants to.

If she even can.

It takes one look from him for her to know she won't. That she doesn't have to.

She remembers how they moved through the house. She remembers how fast and light and limitless she felt.

It takes his touch, his planning, the world's most casual brush of his thumb to remind her: she's always been this woman. And it's always been enough.

✒

Nate undresses her with the same certainty he used to have in his hands, before years of late-night diaper changes and tiptoeing around sleeping toddlers stripped him of it. They tremble as he pulls her shirt over her head, then settle once he feels the softness of her skin, the expanse of it, all the room there is for his touch.

Claire shivers. She loves the cold on her skin, but his fingertips more. She loves how he sets her on her side, curved like a question mark, only bent until she's unfolded and flat. Her breathing is fast, then steady. Her hair is down and loose and wild.

This is what she wanted.

This is what she wants.

Every touch seems to leave an imprint on her. A ghost of his hand lingers, burns and ignites, even when he moves to the next part, the next inch of her, hungry to find a way to touch everywhere, to touch at once. His fingertips graze her skin, brush along her shoulder, then slip to her breast. He takes his time, not impatient but careful. He follows the lines of her body, a path of goosebumps and shivers left in his wake.

It is everything she imagined, before they had babies, when they only had time and newness and themselves.

The air is chilly. Claire can feel it against her legs, her thighs. Nate kisses her stomach, his beard a wonderful roughness, a wonderful grit that she used to pull on and grab when she needed him closer. It's getting too long again. It's exactly long enough.

The tips of his fingers find the hem of her pants. He is slow but deliberate, a push and a tug that leaves her lower half as exposed as the rest. She should be embarrassed. But there is a steadiness in him that holds her together, that lets her want it, want him, want this. Every moment is electric.

It is everything she imagined, before they lost it, when it was a memory.

Nate sets her on her side. He is less gentle than he is certain, knowing exactly what they want. He positions her with the assurance she craves: one leg bent and the other over his thigh. Curved like a question mark, bent until unfolded and flat. Bent until hers. Hers again. Hers now.

Claire's body is open to him, every inch available, a blank canvas he can paint his praise across. She does not mind. She only wants more. The air is cold against her skin. Nate is warm beside her, warm everywhere.

There is pressure in the way he holds her, a heaviness that has nothing to do with weight. His palm rests on her hip, grips with a force that keeps her together. Like he's afraid she will come apart from needing too much or wanting too much or holding it in. Like she's already begun to fall apart, already unfolding, even before they've started. His other hand finds its way to her hair.

She cannot remember him this sure of her since the first time he said I love you.

It is everything she imagined, before she stopped hoping for it, when they were in cars and parks and each other.

Nate lets her get used to the vulnerability of the position, to the exposure, the unlikeliness of it. Then he reaches for the drawer, not waiting or wasting time. He picks out the plug, small but a little more than last time, the familiarity of it almost shocking in the same way as the last time, too. Claire's heartbeat jumps and trips and skips with anticipation. She isn't nervous, not like before, not like when this was new and unfamiliar.

It is everything she imagined, before he came home today, before he even walked in the door.

He coats the toy with lube, careful and precise, the same way he handled her wedding band when it slipped from her fingers down the drain and he saved it, unbent, exactly as it was before. He handles her with that same delicacy. She is almost trembling, almost desperate.

"Okay?" he asks, finally speaking, finally breaking the crackling tension of the room. His voice is low and focused.

"Yes." Her answer is shaky, throaty, raw with want.

He touches the tip of the plug to her ass. It is everything she wants, everything she needs, a sweetness and a heaviness, a familiar, delicious stretch. She presses back, not having to be careful anymore, not needing to ease herself into it.

The toy goes deeper and deeper, the fullness overwhelming. The way she wants.

The way she's learned to need.

Claire breathes deep, thighs already shaking with the intensity. Nate's other hand slides down between her legs, finds her, makes it more than she can handle, more than she can hold together. A moan escapes her lips. She does not even try to stop it. The noise is as raw and honest as the slickness, the slide of his fingers that stokes the heat in her core. It is unrelenting. Perfect.

"Like that," he says, and there's a gruff, possessive sound in his voice, a beautiful praise. A reminder. "So fucking hot."

He pushes the toy deeper, working it inside her with slow but deliberate motions. She cannot stop herself from trembling, from shaking, from getting so wet, she's not sure where she begins and where he does. Claire gasps, air almost too much to hold on to.

But she's not afraid she will come apart. Not this time. This time, she is ready for it. This time, he knows exactly how far to push, exactly how much she can take.

He has watched her, held her, every step of the way.

The plug seats itself inside her, and she moans loudly at the fullness, at the utter perfect tension of it. She does not care how she sounds. She loves how she sounds. Nate strokes her until she's already on the verge of a climax, on the edge of her control.

"Fuck," she gasps, almost surprised by her own body, by the force of it.

Nate steadies her wrist, pulls her closer, holds her in place as he positions himself. As he moves the hand that isn't holding her to his cock. As she hears the way he groans when he grips himself, the sound of it leaving her breathless. Leaving her whole. She trembles, feels the head of him against her entrance, anticipation an ache and a pleasure at once. She never thought she would want anything this much again.

But here she is, here he is. This is everything.

He pushes inside her, slowly, not wanting to rush, savoring the sound of her as much as she savors the sound of him. She is taking all of it, every inch, the length of him buried deep, then deeper, stretching her like the toy, but sweeter, bigger, so much more, so much more. Claire's body opens to him and he watches, like he wants to see everything. Like he needs to.

The dual sensation is almost too much to take.

Almost.

He fills her, a second incredible pressure, moving in her with every stroke, every wordless promise. She gasps and moans, sounds she didn't know she still knew how to make, sounds she has remembered in notes app journals and dreams and wishes and prayers. His eyes never leave her face, fixed on her pleasure, on her control and lack of it. Her softness. Her power.

He tells her how good she is. He tells her to take it.

And she does. She does.

It's everything she imagined, even now.

The world feels small and far away. A pinhole universe. Claire is close enough to see the freckles on Nate's nose, close enough to see the curls of his hair. The sweat. The desire.

Everything tightens and condenses and spins around them, faster than she can take in, faster than she can keep hold of. She doesn't know which way is up, which way is down, which way is yes and yes and more. The pressure builds, crashes, becomes its own breath, becomes the only breath there is. She cries out with everything in her, cries out as it all goes quiet. As it all goes bright.

They have her surrounded. She is too full. It is too much, everything she ever wanted. Her senses are so overloaded, it circles back and she feels like she's floating, the plug in her ass, his cock at her entrance, Nate inside her completely. It should make her burst, but it doesn't. Instead, she expands. She is orbiting everything, crashing into herself and losing control and finding it. She doesn't want it to stop. She needs it to keep going, for Nate to keep going.

He starts with slow, controlled thrusts. He starts by letting her gasp and want and take him, every part of him. His eyes are fixed on her face, like the rest of the world could disappear and he wouldn't notice. Like she's the only thing there is to notice. His gaze is the same pressure as his body. It is the same stretch and insistence and perfect overwhelming.

He is the rock she breaks herself against.

"God, yes," she cries, too needy to say it any quieter, any other way. The force of it all spins her. She doesn't know which way is up. Which way is breath. Which way is please, don't stop, and he doesn't.

She cannot think. She can only take.

Claire feels how he is holding back, waiting for her to unfold again, to take more, take it all. His hips roll, a steady rhythm, each thrust long and precise and perfectly slow. He lets her open and wrap herself around him, stretch with every movement. Every small, deliberate motion of his body feels as big and wide and as infinite as the space between the stars.

She does not want it to stop.

She cannot think. She can only want.

He increases his pace, holds her tight and tighter, her body a trembling softness under the strength of his. A deep, raw moan escapes her lips as he rocks into her, breath and release and relief. Claire's senses are overloaded. Her mind is overloaded. She loses herself in the dual intensity of it, in the heady fullness of Nate inside her, in his thrusts and his hands and his words. She loses herself and finds herself and loses herself.

"Oh, fuck," she moans, no need to hide it, not anymore. "Nate. Yes."

She can barely catch her breath.

She is still everything.

She is still so much.

He holds her steady as she shakes uncontrollably, and he's groaning with her, a beautiful sound, a sound she craves as much as he craves the same from her. She hears the slickness between them. She feels the pulsing heat of him.

She wants this forever.

Her body vibrates with it, her body shakes with it, every stroke threatening to make her come apart. But Nate is there, a steady pulse, steady words, even as his breath becomes ragged and quick. He fucks her harder, the two points of pressure collapsing in on her until they're the only thing there is, the only thing she knows.

The pressure builds. Builds again.

And she begs.

"Don't stop," she cries, almost helpless, almost lost, almost more than she can handle. She feels it at the edge of her senses, a threat, a promise, an ache. She is so close. So close.

"Fuck, Claire," he says, and she feels him everywhere. Every inch of him, every inch of her, no space, no holding back.

She is everything she imagined. Even now.

The pressure builds. It builds.

He is the rock she can dash herself against. He is the rock. She is the sea. She is the world. She is the only thing in it.

Her climax crashes through her with an explosive force. Her legs shake, and her arms shake, and every part of her she thought she knew, she thought she had figured out, comes apart and folds back together, tighter and smaller and brighter. She sobs with the release. Shattering. Utter relief.

Her cries fill the room as she lets go of years of wanting, years of being more, more, more. It is a long and hard unraveling. It is everything.

Nate wraps his arms around her, not letting her go, holding her tightly as she feels the world spin and catch, holding her as she trembles, as she lets it happen, as she lets it be. He is still inside her, and the sweetness of it is more than she thought she could take. But she's taken so much already, and she can take even more.

The aftershocks echo through her.

His voice is low and soothing and thick with emotion.

"Beautiful," he says, words that make her start to shake all over again. "Fuck, Claire. Fuck. Yes."

He holds her tightly, protecting her as she sobs against him, her face buried in his chest, buried in his steady heart, the only steady thing she knows. The only thing that makes sense, when everything else falls away.

Her emotions spill over, but she doesn't feel embarrassed. She doesn't feel the need to keep it in, hold it tight, let it unravel in secret or not at all. Nate's protective embrace makes her feel like she can let it all go. It is a freedom, pure and dizzying. The orgasm leaves her exhausted but liberated. Years of tension and worry and restraint fall away.

She is everything she imagined, even now. Especially now.

And so much more.

She clings to him, his arms a harbor, his warmth a home, his praise and his touch and the way he stays inside her until she knows, really knows, she is everything he wants, and he is everything she needs.

Sheets tangled beneath her thighs. His chest rising, falling beneath her ear. They remain wrapped around each other, bodies too connected to tell where hers begins, where his ends. Where hers ends, where his begins.

Nate kisses her temple softly, a warmth, a tenderness that brings her to tears, brings her out of herself. She is crying for real, too, tears that wet his chest, sobs that are filled with love and years and utter, unfiltered release.

It's the first time Claire has felt like this since they began this journey.

The first time she's felt free since it ended and began and ended and began and ended again.

The first time.

The first.

# Ten

The residue of their encounter is vivid, searing, impossible to shake. Claire moves through the morning on unsteady legs, her body rebelling with every bend, reach, and twist. Even mundane things are colored by the intensity of it, and the sharp shock of desire haunts her every step.

Making breakfast, she remembers his mouth. Folding laundry, she feels the mark of his hand, his grip like a promise. The stretch, the weight, the trembling aftermath—they're all still with her, humming beneath the surface, blurring the edges of her reality with sharp, searing want.

She shuffles from the bedroom to the kitchen, her skin prickling at the whisper of clothes against her body. Claire moves through the morning on unsteady legs, her body rebelling with every bend, reach, and twist. The kids are in high chairs, their little hands demanding cereal and bananas, but she can't stop thinking about the insistent pull of him, the way she came apart with his weight pinning her down. Her fingers shake as she pours milk into a bowl, and she remembers how he filled her, the stretch almost too much and exactly enough.

It all bleeds into the present, staining the ordinary with shades of last night. He holds her open. He holds her down. His hands claim and own and worship. Her breath hitches, the sound lost beneath the kids' babble.

She feels it everywhere—his touch, his words. More. She chokes on a laugh that sounds too much like a sob and looks around, as if someone might have seen or heard, but it's just her and the kids, their chatter as oblivious as it is loud.

The dining room table is littered with papers, bills she meant to sort last night. She gathers them in an unfocused heap, Nate's ghostlike presence woven into every gesture. She imagines him watching her now, that quiet way he does—like he knows she's still aching for him. Like he can feel the echo of how she shook beneath him, the tremors lasting long after they've melted into the sheets, their bodies collapsing and her voice hoarse and foreign in her own ears.

Breakfast is a blur, and she's not sure which one of them wanted more in the end. Her body has never felt so full, her mind never so completely undone. She's quick with the food, the cleanup, trying to stay ahead of the mess her mind is making. But every movement feels new, her limbs fluid and heavy, a pulse at the core of her where his fingers teased and stretched and filled.

She collects toys from the floor, her chest tightening at the sight of the closed laundry room door. How close it had been—immediate and animal, her cheek pressed to the dryer. They hadn't even bothered to leave the lights off. It should have felt cold, rushed, dirty. But instead, it was hot and alive, and she had cried out with it, the release intense and sweet. He'd been everything she wanted, even when she didn't know she could have it. She fumbles with a basket of unfolded clothes, a plush dinosaur tumbling to the floor in her wake.

On autopilot, she gathers the mail from the front step. A breeze lifts the hair off her neck, its touch both cooling and too close. She shivers, everything amplifying the deep tremor still vibrating through her. She never thought she'd feel like this again. Never dared. That it had started with a quick, filthy fuck in the laundry room seems impossible. That it had ended with her wrists tied to the headboard, his breathless more a benediction, feels like something out of the secret journal she'd never planned to share. Yet here she is, glancing at her bare wrists, the absence of marks both surprising and disappointing.

Her arms strain as she picks up one child, then another, her body resisting like it doesn't recognize itself. She clutches them too tightly, afraid she'll drift away if she doesn't anchor herself. The routine feels off, warped by the power of everything she can't stop replaying. She tries to stay in the moment, tries to keep from wandering back to last night's gasps and sighs and shattering release. But every diaper changed, every shirt buttoned, carries the imprint of Nate's touch, and she's helpless against the swell of it.

She sits the kids down to play, and the toys don't hold their attention nearly as long as they used to. She watches their restless movements, finding her mind unwilling to stay still, even as her body wants to collapse under the weight of it all. Her head swims with more than she can hold. Her wrists. His hands. The hot stretch of submission, the release of letting go completely. The urge to chase it, run from it, give into it again and again.

Through the blur of noise, Claire catches sight of her neighbor across the street—Mrs. Leung, out watering her potted tulips, pausing mid-spray to offer a knowing wave. Claire waves back, but the gesture sticks in her throat. There's a flicker in the woman's eyes, the kind that says: I see you. Not as a mother. Not as a mess. Not even as tired. Just you. The version of you that you thought was long gone.

It's startling—a glimpse of someone she thought long buried. She wonders if the change in her is visible to everyone, or if only she can feel the crackling urgency beneath the surface. She tilts her head, imagining the woman she was last night. The woman Nate made her.

He takes her until she cries out. He holds her as the tremors fade. And the secret of it, the vivid stretch and pull, makes the everyday world blur at its edges.

Her days have felt repetitive, a string of unending routine, until now. Until she feels her old self pushing through. Unsteady, newly awakened, a little unraveled—but there, pulsing beneath everything. Claire watches herself in the mirror, caught between disbelief and raw need. Her fingers find the thin chain at her neck, tracing it, wishing it were his grip. He did this to her, for her. The idea sings through her, fierce and feral, making her wonder what comes next.

She stands at the edge of the room, soaking in details. The way they move, talk, laugh—it's new to her, something she hasn't noticed before. Not like this. The room feels different too, the precision of it striking in a way that's both thrilling and unsettling.

Their words carry the sharpness of awareness, secrets traded under the cover of more acceptable conversation. But she can feel it. Claire. Every look. Every joke. Every sideways glance that lands too close to her own heart. It's a challenge and a revelation—her face flushing beneath the weight of it. She tells herself she can handle it, but the doubt lingers as the wine flows and the laughter swells. Even as she turns away, pretending not to feel exposed, the bite of it lingers like the taste of cheap chardonnay.

Naomi's home is artful and intimidating, every piece in place, every surface calculated for effect. Claire's last to arrive, her face still flushed and skin still tingling. She sees them all with fresh eyes—Harper's sharp gaze as she sizes up the room; Brielle's restless shift from the couch to the floor and back again; Rachel's vacant stare into her wine glass, the faraway look of someone who's here but not here at all. The contrast between Naomi's elegant precision and Claire's own frayed interior lands heavily, but there's comfort in the chaos that's missing here. The immaculate order makes her wonder if everyone feels as exposed as she does. She doubts it.

"Look who finally made it," Naomi calls, ushering Claire in with a glass of wine before she's even through the door. Her smile is knowing, like she's already in on a secret Claire hasn't confessed. "We were about to send out a search party."

Brielle flops down beside Harper, stretching like a cat, all limbs and muscle. "We thought you might have gotten tied up."

"Tied up?" Rachel's head snaps up, mascara ad eyes bright with interest. "Or just worn out?"

They all laugh, even Claire. But it's shaky, uncertain, and the room spins around her as she lowers herself to the couch. She can feel their eyes on her, the too-innocent curiosity as they take in the flush that won't leave her cheeks, the way she avoids looking any of them in the eye. The words aren't spoken, but she hears them anyway, echoing last night's thoughts, last night's gasps. There's more than one way to feel full. It shouldn't make her pulse race like this, but it does.

She tries to distract herself, focusing on the tiny details that fill the pristine living room. Monogrammed coasters. Wine bottles lined up like trophies. Matching throw pillows arranged just so. Claire picks one up, clutching it to her chest like a shield, and the secret hums against her skin, frantic and uncontained. She wonders if it shows, if they see it, sense it, and she feels something like panic rising in her throat.

The conversation is fast and loud and everywhere, ricocheting from daycare drama to nap refusals to whether the latest episode of their reality TV obsession is better than last season. Claire nods along, inserting the occasional "Yeah, I know!" and "Can you believe that?" to cover the distance she can't quite bridge. She knows this rhythm, the constant chatter, but tonight it feels different. There are cracks she hasn't seen before, and the perfect facade isn't as seamless as it used to be.

Rachel takes a long sip from her glass, her mouth twisting in a wry smile. "Double trouble," she says, her words cutting through the rest. "Now there's a concept I could get behind."

Claire freezes, her wine glass suspended halfway to her lips. Her grip on the pillow tightens. Her face burns, too slow to hide it, too unguarded to pretend she didn't hear. The other women dissolve into laughter, a shrill and dizzying chorus.

"Claire?" Harper says, eyes narrowing with the kind of focus that can pin a person to the wall. "You okay?"

"What?" Claire forces the word out, but it sounds strangled and foreign.

"You looked…" Harper pauses, watching Claire squirm beneath the weight of their collective attention. "Familiar with the concept."

The laughter swells, and Claire is caught in the center of it. It's not unkind, but it feels like an unraveling, her insides turned out for everyone to see. She fumbles for a response, her voice too bright, too brittle. "You're ridiculous," she says, trying to match their teasing with a smile that's all nerves and no substance. Her hand shakes as she downs the rest of her wine.

Brielle shoots her a grin, more feral than friendly. "Only a little," she says. "But I'm not the one who's all tied up, remember?"

It lands like a direct hit, and Claire knows she won't last the night. She doesn't think they'll let up. The pressure of their awareness is a vise, and the secret that felt thrilling and untouchable now feels precarious, on the verge of slipping through her fingers and into the light. She sets down her empty glass and rises, the room tilting around her.

Naomi reaches for the bottle, already pouring another round. "Leaving so soon? We haven't even gotten to the part where Rach explains exactly how she plans to pull off double trouble."

"We can't have that." Claire grabs her coat, forcing a laugh that's not fooling anyone. "Next time, I promise."

"Are you sure?" Naomi asks, the edge of a challenge in her voice. "You know you can tell us anything, right?"

Claire nods, backing toward the door. "I know," she says, and it comes out like an apology.

She's gone before they can press further, the laughter trailing after her like a physical thing, wrapping her in a cocoon of dread and desire and the very real fear that it won't stay secret for long.

✒

The glow of the screen is too bright in the dark room. She stares at it, words blurring as her mind cycles through everything she didn't say at dinner. She's teetering on the edge of revelation, the secret too big and alive to contain.

Their voices echo in her head—encouraging, teasing, every shade of possible judgment—until she doesn't know what she should say or if she should say anything at all. Even next to Nate, she feels alone, the distance between them an expanse she thought they'd finally crossed. She types words, deletes them, starts again, watching them appear on the screen like small confessions. She could tell them. She almost does. But uncertainty chokes her. She leaves it vague, safe. She puts the phone down, curling into herself, feeling the gravity of keeping a secret that might break her in ways she's only just begun to mend.

The evening stretches out, marked by the empty space beside her on the bed, the space that feels wider with each passing minute. Nate is in the shower, and Claire sits against the headboard, fingers hovering above the keyboard. The silence should comfort—a reprieve from laughter and noise—but it presses in, magnifying her hesitance.

The phone buzzes, the screen flashing with a new message from Rachel. It taunts her from the nightstand until she picks it up again, unable to resist the pull. Her heart sinks—earlier embarrassment sharp, still fresh.

No, she wants to say. No, it's not you. It's me, with all the baggage I didn't know I had. Me, with the secret that feels both enormous and fragile, a secret I didn't know I'd have to keep from even myself. But she doesn't type any of that. Not yet. The pressure is heavy, suffocating, and she blinks against the screen's harsh light, wishing she could blink away her doubts too.

The conversation replays in her head—her fake confidence, the too-bright way she played along. The way it fell apart beneath their looks, their comments, until she was raw and transparent and too close to shattering.

Nate returns, hair damp and face soft with the haze of almost-sleep. "Everything okay?" he asks, sliding into bed and curling around her, his warmth both a balm and a reminder of everything she hasn't said.

She nods, but it's a lie. A lie that only multiplies when Naomi's text lights up the screen:

Mom Club Confidential

Thurs Mar 7 9:58 PM

Rachel

Okay seriously. Did I say something wrong?

Naomi

We're all tired. Some of us just have... glowier reasons.

Claire's laugh is strangled, more like a gasp. "Not that you'd notice," she mumbles, setting the phone aside long enough to turn out the lamp.

"Notice what?" Nate's voice is low and careful.

"Nothing," she says too quickly, feeling the prickle of his gaze in the dark.

"You sure?"

The question lingers, as much about the silence between them as it is about the phone. "I'm sure," Claire whispers, not sure at all. Her hand closes over the screen again, drawn to it like an addict to a fix.

She types a quick, her thumb poised over the send button. But it feels dishonest, even to her. Worse than keeping it a secret is pretending the secret doesn't exist. Her chest tightens with the weight of it, and she presses send before she can change her mind, before she can convince herself it's better to stay silent.

The messages come fast, each one hitting like a small blow, each one tugging at the things she's barely begun to accept. Brielle is first, supportive and familiar. She reads it twice, three times, the words jarring in their kindness.

Claire

It's not like that

Brielle

Claire. Babe. It literally is like that. And we're proud.

Harper

And maybe a little jealous.

Naomi

You know you can tell us anything, right?

A thousand implications swim in the silence between each word, and Claire imagines Harper's cool gaze cutting through every single one.

She starts to reply, her thumbs moving faster than her heart can follow. It is like that. They're right, all of them, and she could say it, confess it, feel the exhilaration of being understood. It's what she wanted, isn't it? What she left dinner craving—the solidarity, the sense that she's not alone, not crazy, not the only one bursting with unspoken things. The thing she wanted more than anything, but not like this.

Her fingers tremble above the keyboard, then fall away.

Claire's breath catches, suspended between fear and relief. It's an invitation and a challenge, a reminder of the laughter and her escape. Of how raw and thrilling it had been to almost spill everything, and how scared she still is.

Some things aren't ready to be said out loud yet. She types it, reads it back, and feels the truth of it stinging. Claire hesitates, the pause stretching out as the phone casts its accusing glow. Then she sends it, shutting her eyes as though she can block out what she's done. Or failed to do.

She places the phone face-down, plunging the room back into darkness. But it's not as dark as it should be. There's a new distance, bigger than before, and it stretches between her and Nate like the gulf of unspoken things. Claire turns onto her side, pulling the blanket up and over and around.

She tries to shake the feeling she's pulled away from everyone she'd just started to let in. The secret still hums inside her—hot, bright, alive—but now it feels like a wedge, not a spark. She thought silence would protect it. But maybe silence is how it dies. Maybe hiding is how she loses everything she's only just begun to find.

# Eleven

She is floating again, adrift in the space between before and after, between trembling anticipation and something bigger than release. Their bed, warm with her husband's scent, cradles her while she drifts—never farther, never gone.

The night buzzes with quiet energy, every shadow reminding her what they've done and what they haven't yet. Claire finds his hand in the dark and tugs him from the edge of sleep. His breath hitches. Her whisper lands like breath in his ear: "Restrain me." Nate's eyes flicker open, a storm pulling itself across his face. "Fill me again," she says. "Don't stop unless I beg." His pupils dilate, and she swears she feels the desire rise off him like heat from sunbaked asphalt. He doesn't hesitate. Doesn't ask if she's sure. Instead, his voice comes out like gravel, rough and low. "Safe word is still red. Got it?" A single nod is her answer. A promise. She watches him get up, retrieve the soft cuffs and the worn leather box that holds everything they've only begun to imagine. He lays them beside her like offering. Like prayer. Then the first press of his mouth, light and undemanding, to the fragile skin at her wrists. Her chest. Her inner thigh. By the time he slips the fabric over her eyes, she is not floating; she is gone.

The room pulls tight around her, no space between her need and his. Claire can almost see the energy buzzing off his skin, his want pouring into her like bright white noise. He presses a kiss to the inside of her wrist, delicate as wings, as breath. His mouth is on her forearm next, working up to the crook of her elbow. She almost doesn't notice the soft leather tightening until it's already done, pulling the tendons beneath her skin taut. When he moves to the other arm, she gasps. His low chuckle feeds the flame unfurling in her belly.

"Good?" he asks, eyes scanning her face, reading her. Knowing her.

"More than," she manages to say.

The room is muted, blurred, full of shadow and shape. Claire hears the click of another cuff and feels it looped, cool and certain, around her ankle. She waits, pulse heavy in her throat, for the next. "Nate," she breathes, and it is all she can do not to lift her hips toward him, toward where she needs him most.

"Tell me if it's too much." His voice is rough now, rasping, half command and half question.

"It's not enough." Her chest is bare, rising and falling with every slow inhale. The cuffs are snug but not uncomfortable—restraints that look more like jewelry than bondage. She tugs against them anyway, testing. Wanting.

He pushes her knees up and apart.

"Yes." The word slips out like a breath she's been holding too long.

"Say it again."

"Yes, yes, please, yes."

He lowers his mouth to hers, catching the sounds and swallowing them, warm and wet. She arches up to meet him, head swimming with need, with how badly she wants this. The loss is abrupt and acute when he pulls away, his hands trailing down her torso with intentional slowness.

Her skin follows, heat chasing his hands. A whimper cuts the air as he moves further, further, too far away.

"Touching isn't stopping," he says, and the spark in his eye matches the one lighting her up inside. He pauses at her knee, spreads her wider still. Then he's right there, hovering above the place that's beginning to throb with his name. He just looks at her for a moment, his breath moving the soft hairs below her belly button, and she feels herself start to tremble. It's a deep, unexpected thing, this vulnerability. A thing she thought she'd fear, but all it does is leave her desperate for more. He kisses her, low and then lower. Between her thighs, across her hip bone.

Then: "You're so good, Claire. So, so good for me."

She can hear the reverence in his voice. It makes her dizzy. It makes her head light and her body heavy with all the ways he touches her next: his hands skimming every exposed inch, the fabric of his shirt grazing her nipples until they're hard, achy, the sweep of his tongue between her breasts, her ribs, her pelvis. She's wet already, he must know, he must see.

"I don't know if I can last," she admits, and it's a confession and a plea, a shiver of anticipation that leaves her craving and craving and craving. He laughs against her skin, and her moan breaks out.

"You don't come until I say," he whispers, and his words are a flood, washing over her, pulling her under.

The blindfold is dark, the room even darker. She is feeling, feeling, feeling. There's no before and after, no tonight and tomorrow. There is only Nate's hands and his mouth, filling every space until it blurs into an endless throb of yes and more and now. Until she is nothing but breath and body and the bite of the restraints against her skin.

She remembers the first time, the next, the time after that—each encounter hotter, hungrier, stretching further into her quiet limits. She remembers nights that went on until morning, with him exploring and teasing, never stopping, even when she was sure she was too spent to want anything else. “Oh god, oh fuck, I need—” The words fly from her, uncontrolled, her spine arching until she can’t feel anything but his mouth, his tongue, the weight of him all around.

“You asked for this, remember?” he says, and she’s almost mad at how easily the chuckle catches in his voice, but there’s no room for anything except fire. She nods, gasps, stretches. Then he’s inside her, two fingers at first, maybe three, so full, so filling. The leather bites into her wrists and ankles, and she has never loved him more. “All of this,” he adds, “and I haven’t even fucked you yet.”

Claire is floating, she is falling. His fingers move faster, deeper, knowing exactly how to make her fall apart. “Oh god, Nate, I can’t—”

“You can.” He says it so firm, so certain, that she almost believes him.

“Please,” she gasps. “Please.”

“Say what you need.”

“Need you,” she pants. “Need to come.”

“Not yet.”

“Nate,” she cries, and it’s a broken sound. The wreck of a woman so close to wreckage.

She wants to be filled. Taken. Destroyed by him. She wants his mouth and his cock and the way he touches her like there’s nothing else in the world he could possibly want. She wants to be gone for him, always and never and again. Her sobs are almost laughter as his fingers still, pause, hold her right on the edge of herself. “Please, I need—”

He slides out of her and back in, rough now, relentless—she doesn’t even know if it’s his fingers, his cock, or both.

“More,” she gasps.

“Everything.”

And he gives it.

She wants to be gone, wants to be wrecked by him. She wants to be all of his.

He pulls out, fills her with the plug, a toy she's loved and hated and loved again, her body stretching to make room for its girth. Her breath goes ragged. His does too. She is slick, so wet, ready for everything he gives. He presses into her with his cock and oh, she thinks, oh, oh, oh, as he fucks into her and keeps on fucking. She is too full, too empty, too everything. The feeling of him all the way inside, right there, relentless and precise, makes her dizzy. She tugs against the cuffs, against the edges of herself, pushing and pulling and never wanting to stop.

He kisses her throat, swallows her sounds.

"I've got you," he breathes, and the words rip her open. He holds her there, on the edge of herself, on the edge of this unending wanting, her nerves raw and electric. Her chest tightens. Her vision blurs. She's going to come, she's going to break, she's going to—

"Oh my god," she gasps. "Oh my god."

"Not yet," he says again, and it's a growl and a tease and a promise she knows he'll keep. She arches into his words, into him, into how sure he is that she can take more.

The plug inside her sends jolts across her body. Nate's fingers find her clit and circle it, relentless and perfect, keeping her right there, hovering, a wire about to snap. She's so full she could burst. So close she could die. He thrusts harder, his cock pushing and pulling, making her gasp, her muscles taut as cables.

Then: "Now."

And her world shatters.

His voice hits her with the force of a breaking wave, and it's everything she needs, everything she wants, how he's always been. Always been for her. She comes, fierce and unending, her voice breaking on a cry, his name, please and yes and more. She comes, the toy still filling her, his cock still inside, too much and not enough and more than she's ever known to want. She comes, and he never stops. Her heart shakes loose from its mooring, free and crashing, each pulse like the first, like the last, like everything she didn't know she needed. It's a wrecking, it's a rebirth, it's too deep and too good and everything all at once. It's everything and more, and it is never, ever going to end.

She comes, and she cries.

The blindfold lifts. She sees white stars, white heat, white nothing, like she's about to faint or fly apart or die or more. Her body trembles in aftershock, a storm she's barely beginning to weather. Nate stays inside her, still and unmoving and a lot like love. She breathes hard, chest heaving, the last shudders breaking through her like tiny live wires.

Then she is aware of his voice, soft as snowfall, blanketing her world. "More?" he asks, and the answer is already written on her skin: need and yes and again. She's never been stretched this thin, never felt so filled, so unmaking and urgent, like they're digging up the past six years and finding who they used to be. She's never had his cock and his patience at the same time. Never had this. The first slow thrust brings her back to the edge of it, reminds her how it feels to be alive and wanting. She tips her head back, lets the world unfurl in unending waves. Lets Nate's cock unfurl her the same way. Then she's not aware of anything. Then she's everything.

The first thrust is everything she remembers and everything she's forgotten in the minutes since he made her cry. He fills her up so full she can't breathe around it, and she loves him for how far he's willing to push, for the limits he knows and the ones he doesn't yet. Her hands strain against the cuffs, and she gives herself over. Her voice breaks like light against a cracked pane of glass: "Nate." He sounds out her name too, low and hoarse, almost feral with wanting her like this, raw and unfurled. The next thrust is slow, then slower, then so fast she sees stars again, and they're streaking and screaming and heat and oh god, she thinks, oh god, he's going to. And he does. He's unrelenting and careful, overwhelming and in control. He takes her apart and puts her back together again and again, until there's no beginning or end to how good this is. Her body opens for him—every desperate inch an open-ended promise. He doesn't say a word, but she hears him loud as gunshot. I've got you. I love you. Don't stop.

The blindfold is wet when he removes it. She hadn't even realized.

"What if I can't," she says, and it comes out more like a question, more like a challenge.

"You can," he says, never hesitating, and his fingers slide between her legs to remind her how it felt just moments ago, how he had her teetering on the edge of herself, how they almost had to stop because she was sure she'd split in two from wanting. "More?" he asks again, but it's not really a question.

"Yes," she breathes, already, still. "Always."

Claire is shaking. She's shivering from how good it is, how much she wants, how his patience fucks her even harder than his cock does. Her pulse is loud in her ears, heavy as a warning, soft as a lullaby. His cock is even heavier. Each time it hits, she sees new colors, brighter colors, colors that don't exist in any world but the one Nate's giving her. She is high on the last orgasm, low on breath and sanity. High and low, high and low, everything stretching and releasing, new galaxies as she unravels for him. It's too big for one woman. Too big for this woman. Too big, but oh god, please don't stop.

His fingers circle her clit. His fingers fill her ass. His fingers lace through hers. Her cuffs are too tight. His hands aren't enough. She needs him to hold her, even while he fucks her, even while she's stretched this thin and ruined. She needs all of him, every single inch, and when he gives it, she comes. Her body lights up and burns out, a flare against the black. She doesn't even have time to breathe, to hope, before the next one rolls in like storm waves. Over and over. Then again. He never stops, not even when she goes limp and tight and wrecked, not even when she gasps, "Nate, oh my god, Nate."

She is never, ever going to stop.

Her sobs turn to laughter and back to sobs.

Her body shakes so hard she's not sure it'll ever stop.

Her mind whites out.

Then she cries.

The sound of his voice holds her together, even when it sounds like she's breaking, even when she doesn't know how or why. She cries and she comes, and she knows he'll never let her go.

She's not used to feeling this much. She's not used to being this alive.

"Claire?" he says, softer now. "Claire?"

She isn't floating this time. She's unmoored.

There's no before or after—only the dizzy now, pulsing and vast.

She is trembling again, maybe crying. It's too big. It's too much. It's too perfect, and oh god, please never stop.

She doesn't know what she wants. She doesn't know how to ask.

"Nate," she says, and it's more of a sob than a word, more of a raw nerve than anything.

His arms go tighter around her, but they never once stop fucking. Not until he sees the tears and her coming and he knows, oh god, he knows.

"I—I don't know why I'm crying." Her voice is small and fragile and amazed.

"More?" he asks, but he already knows the answer.

He is the answer.

He is the only one.

He unties her. Wraps a blanket around her. Cradles her like she's made of glass.

"I've got you," he whispers. He always has. He always will. He holds her tight, fucks her slow, until it feels like safety. Until it feels like everything.

"I love you," she says, the words foreign in her mouth—not because they're new, but because she forgot she was allowed to say them out loud.

She needed to break.

To see there was more to her than holding on.

That surrender wasn't weakness—it was proof she'd survived.

Now she's got him too.

Now he never, ever stops.

She cries, but he knows what she really means.

They lie tangled, skin on skin, words unwritten.

Everything left to say.

She lies wrapped in Nate's arms, not just wrecked—but rewritten.

She had to fall apart to find the parts she still wanted.

And here he is, handing them back to her.

One touch at a time.

# Twelve

Claire wakes tangled in sheets, the imprint of him still fresh on her body—like an unfinished sentence. The kids are already screaming, a shrill alarm that sets the day in motion, but all she feels is the press of his hands, the way he covered her mouth when she almost cried out.

She pulls on a loose tank top, pretending not to notice the fingerprints still blooming against her skin. But they're impossible to ignore—the phantom ache, the memory of asking him for more. Downstairs, the noise hits her like a wall. Milk spills across the counter, and she stands in the middle of it all, struck by the secret of their unspoken desire, even as her husband packs a sandwich and doesn't meet her eyes.

When she slips out of bed, the rawness at her wrists whispers of the cuffs—tight, unyielding, yet exactly what she'd wanted. What she'd begged for. The way his mouth had silenced her cries, hungry and unrelenting. Claire hugs her body, feeling the ghost of Nate's hands pressing her down, spreading her wide. She pulls on a clean tee and yoga pants, each fabric brushing the marks he's left, igniting new heat from last night's embers.

The kids scream as she heads downstairs, relentless. A thump, then wailing. Claire barely registers which kid it is. All she feels is the lingering thrill of Nate's hard, deep thrusts. Of being pinned under his raw need.

Milk splatters across the counter. A spoon clatters to the floor. Through it all, Claire stands—part of her still in that dark room where whispered commands turned her gasps into moans, where she thought she might fly apart.

The memory holds her—like he had. His lips trailing down her neck, the grip on her hips, firm and unyielding. The deliberate, knowing pace of his movements, as if each one were designed to push her to new edges. Even now, cleaning up the sticky floor, she hears the echo of herself, wild and desperate and alive. "I asked for that," she'd thought last night, amazed, wanting, as he left her shaking and stunned. "I asked for that," she thinks again now, bare feet wet with milk.

Nate moves through the morning routine, his tired but strong hands making lunch, pouring coffee. The counter is just a counter, except Claire knows what it had been last night. An unspoken challenge. An answer to everything she'd feared lost. She watches him and waits for him to meet her eyes, the weight of it all hanging in the charged air between them.

The kids are relentless, screaming over cereal and spilling juice, but her mind stays caught on the heat of the encounter—the vivid, raw, explicit memory of Nate's mouth on her, of the daring toy that had driven her to beg. How he'd undone her with every touch, left her trembling and marked with the truth of her own desires. She tracks him across the room, his presence as potent as last night's hunger, and wonders if he knows she's already ready for more.

She steps into the laundry room. The scent hits her—fabric softener, heat, memory. The hum of the machine is steady, but it's not what she wants. Her palm grazes the dryer's cool surface, and in a flash, she's back there—pressed flat, his breath on her neck, her own voice lost to the thrum of bodies moving like need. It had been fast and filthy and perfect.

She sinks to the floor beside the basket, the weight of everything settling in her limbs. The towels are warm, but not like him. Nothing is. Every soft fold is a lie—none of it bites the way his grip had, none of it demands like the toy still tucked in the nightstand.

Her body aches like it's still waiting. Still wanting. She closes her eyes and remembers the way he'd claimed her—rough, relentless, reverent. The cuffs. The door locked behind them. The way he made her feel like she could shatter and still be safe.

The machine rattles beside her, echoing the rhythm he set with his hips. She wants it again. Wants him again. But the room is empty. And so is she.

She thought wrecking herself for him would be the answer. That surrendering would bring them closer. But now, in the silence, she wonders if he felt it at all—or if she was the only one coming undone.

In the bedroom, they lie inches apart—his back turned to her. It feels like miles. Her skin remembers the way his hands had been everywhere last night. The room had been silent then too, save for her cries and his gruff commands, the obscene noises of bodies colliding, skin on skin.

Toys left on the bedside table are a graphic testament to how bold he had been. How bold they both had been. But now the air is heavy and wordless, the evidence of desire not quite enough to bridge the gulf. In the quiet, she relives each raw thrust, every slick touch, waiting for him to roll over and pull her close. He doesn't. The glow of her phone lights the room—a poor substitute for passion.

Mom Club Confidential

Thurs Mar 7 10:47 PM

Brielle

Someone please entertain me. My vibrator just died mid-ramp-up. I'm grieving.

Rachel

I would, but I'm too bitter to be funny today.

Harper

Same. Everything's quiet and I don't trust it.

Naomi

Maybe silence isn't golden. Maybe it's a red flag in heels.

Claire

Silence can be the loudest thing in the world..

Claire lies motionless, the distance between them charged and sharp. The evidence of his attention still glistens on her skin, sticky and intimate and a reminder of how completely he'd wrecked her. Of how completely she'd let him.

The cuffs, the toys—he'd brought them out bold and confident. Left them out like a flag planted, proof of their raw, graphic reconnection. But now Nate is turned away, his back a wall she can't breach. She shivers with the memory of his hard, unrelenting thrusts, waiting for him to roll over and pull her close.

His hand had claimed every inch of her. His mouth, too, possessive and filthy in ways that left her spent and shaking, barely able to draw a breath. The silence in the room echoes that fierce, explosive intimacy, a reminder of how forceful he'd been. How gentle. His gruff voice, the pulse of the daring toys, her own body stretched open and trembling under his confident weight. They'd pushed past every boundary. Together. But now there is only the sound of Nate's steady breathing, the heat of last night still clinging to her body, an erotic and agonizing afterimage.

She thought wrecking herself for him might be the answer. That surrendering would bring them closer. But now, in the silence, she wonders if he felt it at all—or if she was the only one coming undone.

She doesn't remember when they'd stopped talking, but she feels it now—the absence of words, even when his hands had filled in every gap. His thumb against her throat, quieting her screams. His tongue finding slick, intimate places, working her until she was hoarse and he was as rough and wrecked as she was. In the dark, she wonders if he's still the same man, desperate to reclaim what they'd lost, or if she's the only one still haunted by those vivid, unapologetic desires. By the image of them both in those wild, naked moments where nothing else mattered. Where no part of her was untouched.

Claire waits, almost holding her breath, expecting him to claim her all over again. But the longer the quiet stretches, the more the distance seems to grow. She replays the way he'd pushed her over the edge, the obscene, explicit connection that had redefined what she thought she could want. Her fingers ache to reach. Her voice aches to ask. In the charged darkness, they're separated by the span of a single bed and everything left unsaid.

The phone glows between them, lighting the space where his arms aren't. A message pops up, jarring and bright. Claire stares at the screen, her breath catching on a bitter laugh.

Claire lets out a small, hollow sound that isn't quite a sob or a laugh. She hovers over the keyboard, unsure of how to answer. Her skin still burns from earlier, her mind a torrent of half-formed thoughts. The afterglow of their explosive, body-shaking intimacy fills her with longing and frustration, a physical need for him to say something, anything. To show her she's not alone in wanting more. The phone dims again, leaving only the quiet and the stubborn space between them.

Claire wonders if Nate's closed eyes hide the same desires, the same struggle. If the gulf she feels is just another temporary ache, like the ones he'd left on her skin. She imagines him reaching for her, pulling her into the hard, solid comfort of his chest, whispering away her doubts the way he'd whispered other, filthier things just hours before.

She is alone with the dark—the echoes of want still vibrating through her skin—and a silence that feels less like peace, more like a dare.

# Thirteen

The notification startles her—an angry pulse of light, like a shaming beacon on Nate's otherwise silent phone. It demands attention. Demands curiosity. Claire should ignore it, but can't. They're not in the habit of secrets anymore. Not since the threads of their marriage caught fire. So she sets aside her unfolded laundry and checks for anything urgent. A slow unraveling follows, then a plunge. Hands trembling, face flushed, stomach wrecked—Claire drops his phone like it burns. The messages are intimate, explicit. They're not from her.

She picks it up again, her heart wild as her eyes move through the digital betrayals. Even now, she doesn't want to believe them. But there they are, damning and undeniable. Words she can't unread.

> I'm dripping wet, baby.
>
> Can't wait until you're inside
> me again.

Text after text, all in a long, unbroken chain. Claire reads the woman's name. She doesn't recognize it. She doesn't need to. It feels like suffocating. Like choking. Her body keeps responding even as her mind races to catch up. The blood at her temples pounds; she hears it loud and rhythmic and hot.

This wasn't supposed to happen—not after everything. Nate was the one who pushed, the one who kept wanting, even when she thought she'd drifted too far to be found. They weren't roommates anymore. Weren't strangers.

They'd just started finding each other again. Just started breathing the same air without bracing.

He had her lock the laundry room door, press her open desire into him like an apology for the silence. It wasn't supposed to happen, but Claire knows what she's seeing. He's given himself to someone else. He was never hers—not really.

Her eyes blur. She keeps scrolling, searching for any explanation, any hint she's misread. They're all from before the wedding, but the words—the wanting—feel raw, fresh, possible. Why's he keeping them? Why's he reading them now? The more she looks, the deeper the impact: seeing each message like a match striking, setting off a flare in her gut, in her chest. What they have isn't real. They haven't rebuilt at all. Her throat tightens; her vision sways. She hears static, half expecting to see it wafting through the monitor with Nate's fucks and his 'baby's'.

She swipes fast, fingers flying over damning evidence. Can't get enough. Can't wait until morning. You make me so fucking hot.

Back to barely holding on.

She imagines him reading these, then touching her with someone else's residue on his hands, on his mouth, inside of him still.

Nothing feels whole.

Nothing feels like hers.

Nate walks in before the tears do, hair wild from work, eyes soft and unsuspecting. Seeing him makes her hate him, makes her heart kick hard against the weight of it. How much is true? How much has he let her believe? Claire stands, shaking, adrenaline stinging every limb. She throws his phone to him like a grenade.

"Who is she?" She spits it, scalding and raw. "Who the fuck is she?"

He catches it. Flips it over. Blanches. She doesn't know if he looks horrified or just caught. Claire watches his mouth open, his voice refuse. "I—"

"Did you fuck her?" She's still burning, words unstoppable, unfiltered, hot as the wreckage inside. "Is this why you've been so… so intense? You were just pretending? Just…" It hits her anew, the fresh wave of old history. "Is this your thing? Turn her on, then tear her apart?"

"Claire. What?" His eyes are wild, as confused as hers are clear.

"You're still keeping secrets, Nate. You're still… you're still a liar!" Her voice splinters. The anger twists and tightens and makes room for hurt. "This whole time, you… you didn't… how could you?"

He holds the phone like it's a bomb. "Where did you find this?"

"I didn't find anything. It lit up." Her arms cross, each breath another fracture. "I thought it was important." She thinks it still is. She thinks it's everything. "I can't believe you've been keeping those." Claire's chest rises, falls, each gasp too big and too small at once. "Who is she, Nate?" She fights the crack in her voice, hates that it finds her first.

He doesn't want to say it. But he's tired of lying by omission.

"They're old." His defenses are paper thin. Claire sees right through. She shoves against them, testing their fragility.

"That's not what I asked." Her chin lifts; her glare catches him square in the unsteady places. She's all accusation, all wound. "Why are they still there?"

Nate's jaw tightens, his arms still limp at his sides. He looks at the messages again, then to her, like maybe there's a question he didn't hear.

"You're overreacting."

"Fuck you." Her breath catches, then breaks. She hears the static again, louder than before. "You were just waiting for me to see this, weren't you? Just waiting until… until you could… Could say you needed someone else?" Her chest heaves, tight with rage. Her eyes are clear with tears. "Say that I wasn't enough again?"

"I didn't want you to see it at all. They're… it's not what you think." His words aren't fast enough. He isn't fighting hard enough to mean them. She's half furious, half terrified he really doesn't want to.

"Then tell me," Claire presses, voice sharp, the fear desperate to stick. "Tell me what it is." She waits, and it burns and burns.

✒

Claire's waiting silence is deafening—louder than her accusations, twice as painful. Nate still holds the phone like it's a truth he didn't want her to see, not this way.

Not while they were just starting to be better. Her anger lands, raw and splitting, but it's nothing compared to the hurt. Nothing compared to the way her words make him believe them. Nate doesn't flinch; he doesn't retreat. He looks right at her, right at everything. "I kept them because it reminded me of us."

He watches it cut her, fast and hard. She folds her arms tight against the blow.

"What's that supposed to mean?" Claire's voice is sharp, suspicion clinging to every word. Her body's less certain—rigid and tender, poised to shatter if he says it wrong. "We're nothing like that."

"That's what I mean." He breathes in, the ache already too familiar. "We used to be." He runs a hand through his hair, pushing back the morning, the years. Pushing back everything—except this.

Her face is still flushed. He wants to be the one to cool it, not cause it. He isn't sure she'll let him touch her again—not after the words already between them. "I kept them because I miss it." His words break and catch, like breathing against the hurt. "Because I miss us."

He looks at her, seeing both the shock and the recognition that's just beginning to pull at the edges of her anger. He looks at her—long enough that she can't look back.

Claire's eyes find the floor, her next breath shaky and sharp. "But we're not… it's not…" Her disbelief curls, then quiets. "Why wouldn't you just tell me?"

Nate holds her gaze, lets the question sit between them. Because you wouldn't want to hear it. Because you didn't want me. Because I was afraid you'd leave if you knew I felt like I already had. The answers pile up, unsaid but not hidden. He touches the phone again, a tangible reminder of the weight he's been carrying. "I didn't know how," he finally says, voice low and stretched thin.

"You didn't know how? Or you didn't want to?" She cuts, then flinches at the wound. Her voice is a shrinking echo of itself. "You'd rather have those than… than try?"

"They weren't my first choice." Nate's tone isn't cruel, isn't kind. It's a simple truth that he doesn't try to hide from her. "They weren't even my second."

The distance feels vast, impassable—like it's been there longer than either of them realized. He wishes he'd closed it sooner. Now, it takes everything he has to cross it. "We didn't even kiss for a year, Claire." He swallows, hard. "You barely saw me. And when you did… you barely looked."

She doesn't say anything. Doesn't have to. Her arms drop, and with them, every defense she'd built.

He takes her silence and cradles it, afraid that's all he has left. "I felt like a ghost." The admission is heavier than he'd imagined, heavier than he thought he could still carry. Nate's shoulders sag; his grip loosens; his hands fall to his sides. They catch on nothing but air.

"You were so far away, and I didn't know how to reach you."

Her knees buckle; she sits. The bed sinks beneath her, and Nate feels the gravity of the distance closing, not fast enough to save them. But enough to see each other across the breach. Enough to make the fall feel real.

"I didn't know you felt like that."

"It was like I was the only one trying."

"We both were," she whispers, small and surprised at the reminder. "I just… I didn't know you were hurting too."

Her voice softens, his sharpens. "I wanted to forget about them, Claire. I wanted it so bad." He feels unsteady, transparent, ripped open in a way that's all new and all the same. "I thought if I just waited, if I kept pretending I was fine…" He shrugs, helpless, still unsure. "Maybe you'd see me again. But it just got worse."

The depth of it stuns her. She doesn't know how to hold any of it yet. He watches her hands find each other, unsure of what to reach for. The quiet turns, a slow and widening circle. She looks at him with a realization he wishes he didn't have to make her see. "So you read them instead?" She sounds sadder now, sad for him, sad for her, sad for everything.

"I'm sorry." He doesn't say it as a promise. He says it because it's all he knows to give.

She blinks. Her anger falters. Her voice softens. "Nate."

"It felt like the only thing left. And even then, I didn't… it wasn't…" He's more exposed than he's ever been. "It never felt like enough." He's ashamed at how much it didn't, ashamed at how much he still hoped for more.

Her arms wrap around her body like a safety net. Like a wish for comfort he didn't think he could give her. She breathes slowly, absorbing his apology and letting it crash into the spaces where anger once settled. "I didn't know you kept all that. I didn't know you wanted it."

"I didn't know if you ever wanted me to."

She studies him, disbelief and sadness lingering in her eyes. They're wide and wet, knowing and still raw. "How could you even think that?" Her question isn't sharp. Isn't accusatory. It's a simple echo of how much they haven't been saying.

"You didn't want anything to do with me, Claire. You stopped choosing us. You stopped choosing me." Nate runs both hands through his hair, unsure if he'll ever stop running. Unsure if she'll ever want to catch him. "I didn't know if it would be different this time. If you really wanted this again, or if..." He braces himself against the risk. "If I'd lose you all over."

She holds the hurt between them, unsure of what it means. But this time, she doesn't run. She doesn't let go. "Why wouldn't you just tell me?"

"I didn't want to hear the answer."

"But what we've been doing..." She trails off, each step another discovery. "Has it even been real?" She's finally asking. She's finally ready.

Nate closes the distance between them. He sits on the bed, the space between them closing. The breath between them shared. It's the closest they've been all day. It still feels too far. "It's the realest it's ever been." He holds her gaze, waits for it to soften. It doesn't, not yet, but it doesn't harden either. "But I was so scared I'd fuck it up. I was so scared you'd go, I couldn't stop myself."

"From keeping them?"

"From holding on to the ghost of us. To the ghost of you." He reaches for her hand; she doesn't move away. But she doesn't move closer, either.

Claire finally lets her shoulders sag, like they're sharing the burden, like maybe it's not just his to bear. "Why didn't you just say you needed this? Needed us?" She watches the sadness lift just enough for him to answer.

"Because it's been too long. Because I didn't want to hear it if you didn't."

"I did." Her voice is small, wounded. So is her smile. "I do."

The hope lands soft, gentle, scared to break. "I want this. More than anything."

"So do I."

They don't kiss, don't fuck, don't burn through the anger and back to the lust like it was a temporary detour. They hold the truth between them. Nate touches the outline of her hand. Claire doesn't let go. They sit apart, quiet—and this time, the silence feels different. They both breathe into it, filling the space they're just starting to see again.

# Fourteen

Claire pauses at the door, listening for proof of life beyond the dim hum of the refrigerator. Then, the quiet stings: the absence of baby static, children's voices, Nate's too-calm count of three. It is a silence that echoes, thumping its way upstairs and slipping under the bathroom door, just cracked enough to tease.

A full bath, lavender plumes dissolving in its heat. She stands, barefoot, as steam fogs her glasses and smudges the edges of a note on the counter. "I packed the kids up. Mom's for the night. —N" He has forgotten his phone. Maybe on purpose. Maybe just another invisible presence that curls around her, floats past her, leaves her.

She stands motionless, a brief inhale held in her chest. Her eyes trace the slant of light that falls from the hallway, creeping over the hardwood like a tentative advance. She is unwilling to exhale, to expand, to occupy space so soon. As if the sound of breath will summon them all back before she has a moment to consider. Claire adjusts her grip on the doorknob, trying to savor the release that should come with solitude. The indulgence of nothing but quiet air and time. But it presses in on her instead, something tight and small that fills her up to the throat.

They are gone for the night. She is here alone, left behind with a house full of her own voice ricocheting off the walls. Claire doesn't know how to feel the noise again once it has stopped.

The quiet echoes back to her in an endless arc, slipping beneath the bathroom door, just cracked enough to tease. A full bath, lavender plumes dissolving in its heat. Steam floats into the hallway, soft as fog and sticky as regret.

He must have known she would find it this way—water brimming over porcelain edges, candle flickering its predictable rhythm against the mirror. Or maybe Nate left before the wax cooled, not wanting to watch it gutter out. Just like the both of them, she thinks, unable to look at each other in the final stretch. Better to avert their eyes than see the moment it snuffs out.

She crosses the threshold and almost closes the bathroom door behind her. Claire isn't sure how to seal herself in with doubt still wedged in the opening. So she leaves a slim piece of doubt wide open.

Her footsteps soften against the tile, the small noises of them overtaken by bathwater slapping at its own surface, an indelicate little thing that bobs and burbles and dares her to take it for granted. She stops short of the sink, as if the folded towel and soap dish will crumble at her trespass. The bath doesn't waver, it doesn't burn out, it doesn't trickle down the drain before she can feel its heat. Claire imagines it is an extension of Nate—just as unfaltering, just as quietly threatening to leave her. She stands still and waits for the steam to rise up and drown her.

Maybe it's a way for him to say what he can't say to her face, maybe just an obligation to fulfill before he disappears. A final exhale before going under. Claire rubs at the fog settling over her lenses, too soft to distinguish between it and tears.

The towel is plush, fresh, the kind that used to linger on Claire's skin after long mornings together—back when they still had mornings together.

Claire remembers the first year they were married. The leisure of early Sundays, the drowsy stretches from bed to bath, how her skin flushed with the morning's warmth, his. How they took time for themselves, together. How Claire knew she was more to him than a woman who dried dishes and folded toddler underwear. How he would catch her at the stove, smiling at the curve of her hip like it was enough to hold the both of them. Now, there is no hip. There is just the tension between him and her and the absence of anything around them.

She doesn't know how to uncoil it.

It used to be an unspoken thing. The way Nate anticipated her needs before she had to voice them, the way he read her as easily as her own handwriting. But even after six and a half years, even after three children, he can still surprise her. And he does. Not with his quiet gesture, but with how easily he can remove himself from it.

He has taken the kids for the night, but he has also taken himself. As much a part of the ritual as the lavender he poured into water.

The strain of the last week catches at the back of her throat, snagged and speechless, tangled up in Claire's attempt to take the breath he left her with. She thinks of Nate's absence in the big, loud way. The abrupt and hollow gap, the missing space where he should be. How the distance between them continues to spool. How neither one of them can untangle it long enough to see what's left. The strain has settled into a dense little thing inside of her, ready to expand or rupture.

She hasn't decided which.

In his rush to get the kids ready, Nate left his phone. It sits on the counter next to a framed family picture, but Claire isn't sure which is more haunting—his reflection or the ghost of his oversight. His phone is a tangible thing she can hold in her hand, her heart. It is a reason for her to doubt him, a reminder that he is just as close and just as impossible to reach.

Steam rises, carrying the ache of its own heat, dropping it like a blanket she didn't ask for.

This bath was meant for Claire. But she wonders, now, if it is the same kind of certainty Nate has for them. Her. A wife. A woman who should take it for granted, even when it unravels.

Claire stands in the middle of the bathroom, the luxury of space that echoes the rest of the house. A little too vast. A little too vacant. She is on her way out when she sees it: the note left on the counter. A blank envelope sheathed in steam, damp at the edges.

It isn't addressed, but Claire knows. It's just like him, like Nate, to make her fill in the blank spaces herself.

She picks it up, light as paper and fear. It weighs down on her anyway, words crumpling her under their tiny pressure: "

I packed the kids up. Mom's for the night. —N

Maybe he wrote it with the pen she always kept for shopping lists and apologies, the one she once used for her designs and sketches. Before.

Claire stands still, breath held, exhale caught. She doesn't know what she should do with this gesture, this goodbye that sits between them in silence. But she stays. Claire stays. She is almost surprised at the finality of her own stubbornness. A coward would have left. A coward would have curled into the absence of them and let it leave her raw. A coward would have left. And Claire almost did.

✒

Claire moves like she's half-asleep, shedding the loose skin of her soft sweater and fuzzy socks, dropping them into a careless pile that seems too hollow and frail to be the sum of her parts. She imagines they are pieces of herself, discarded and irrelevant, without form. The collar of her tee sticks a little as she pulls it over her head. This one had been a clean shirt. Only worn for half of the day. Only half worn out.

Her leggings drag and bunch at her ankles, soft cotton limp around her bare feet. She pictures Nate watching from a distance, cataloguing the slackness of her abandoned clothes with disinterest. How he has watched her for months, barely seeing, barely noticing as she shifts her way into something looser, softer, less composed. This is the only way Claire knows how to change, a slow unraveling that leaves pieces of herself crumpled and thin.

She doesn't know if she can peel away everything else as easily.

She steps into the bath, unsure of how it will hold her.

The steam moves more than she does. It billows and curls and fills the room, a ghostly weightless thing, already more whole than she has been in weeks. Claire hopes she will become that way too. Full. Weightless. Drifting without so much resistance.

But her empty clothes are a stark and still life, stark and still. A woman-shaped heap of unresolved parts. They are pieces of herself that Claire has dropped without care or purpose, the way Nate drops things when they aren't worth holding onto.

Claire holds onto everything. Every slight, every little word, every moment of tense silence between them. She grips it all like an apology waiting to be born, unwilling to exhale until Nate takes it from her himself.

It feels like another way to hurt her. This gesture, this warmth, this whole-cloth thing he has given to her without expecting to get anything back. Claire watches it curl around her like something she might have believed, once, but knows better than to now. He is not here, and it is an unkind and unfailing absence. He is not here, and it is louder than the noise of a full house.

She wants him to notice. She wants him to watch. She wants him to mean it when he does.

When they first got married, he would watch her undress from his spot on the bed, then follow her to the bath with a lazy grin and nothing else. The effortlessness of love made simple, undemanding, shared in the afterglow of hours that had no one else to fill them. He took his time. Claire's, too. Now, she isn't sure where the time goes. The days don't feel like hers, the hours fold into themselves and unravel into tired afternoons of nap schedules and laundry heaps. And Nate, with his ability to step in and out of them with so much grace, so little struggle.

She wants to hate him for that. But Claire is not a woman who knows how to hate.

So she does the only thing she knows how to. She steps into the bath, unsure of how it will hold her.

It takes a moment for Claire to catch her breath. To catch up to it. To let it expand. She lowers herself inch by inch, and she wonders if the water can tell that she has not been this bare for him, for herself, for longer than she remembers. She waits, breath held, body tense, before she lets herself go and submerges completely.

Claire closes her eyes and lets the water swallow her. She tips her head back until her ears fill with the murmur of air escaping, a little darker, a little more viscous than it should be. The candle, the steam, the heat, all of it muted beneath the tiny rise and fall of her own, drowning pulse. Her own, underwater heartbeat. The sound is small, muffled, a small echo that reaches only as far as the house itself.

Even that sound drowns out what should be here, what she should feel, the comfort of knowing he will always be within arm's reach. A steady and invisible thing, unsinkable, but still dragging her down to depths she can't hold her breath through. The effortlessness of love made unspoken, unbearable, adrift. Claire exhales, lets everything go, the kind of long-held breath that only comes at the end of something too short, too incomplete. She lets it go and it makes no difference.

The water closes in around her, impossibly warm. Impossibly alone.

The house is silent, but she can still hear the missing pieces, loud in their echo of an earlier life. Loud in the way that missing him should never be.

Claire opens her eyes to the sound of solitude, to the things she still can't fully see. Her gaze rises to the surface, rippling and restless, the brief outline of a reflection that wavers and distorts before she can get a grip on it. Before it can settle into a true and trustworthy thing.

It makes the quiet sound bigger. His absence sound bigger. And it magnifies everything else until it is almost unbearable. Until Claire wants to rise up and gasp for air, unable to draw any in, unable to expel what sits inside of her with so much heaviness. The silence. The tension. The distance that neither of them knows how to close.

Claire floats to the surface, hoping it will all feel different from the other side of breath. It doesn't. The quiet follows her up, sticks like water and holds her down like doubt. It laps at the edges of a hurt she can't get rid of, no matter how often he tells her to. She's the one who always has to say it first. She's the one who always has to break the surface with the raw, bare way she feels everything. He is just a silent, unsinkable thing.

They don't talk about it. Not about the distance that has been growing.The silence between them in the mornings, the way they orbit each other with new gravity and older bruises, the strain that pulls tighter the further they drift.

They don't talk about how she wanted more than this.

But it sits between them in everything they say. Claire remembers. She remembers the way he looked at her two nights ago, the way he pushed her off like she was an advancing wave. Unstoppable. Threatening. Distant. The memory floats back to her, heavy as guilt.

She had reached for him. He had shut her down, not because he didn't want her, but because he was exhausted. Claire feels the tug of that moment like a rising tide, feels the pull of a husband who only ever goes halfway to meet her.

The bath soothes her like an unexpected ache.

Maybe she went too far. Maybe she asked for more than either of them could handle. Maybe he's giving her space now, a night to think about it. About them. About what it means to need him more than he knows how to need her back.

She lets her body go slack in the cooling water.

Even when he pushes her off, Claire is always the one to say it first. She misses him. She loves him. She doesn't know what that was, but she wants it back. And Nate is the one who drifts into silence, floats into her space when he thinks the worst has passed. She wonders if this is another one of those times. If the bath is an offering, a way for him to say sorry without ever having to, a way for him to stay on the surface while Claire drowns.

She pulls herself out of the water, doubting it's anything but impersonal. Another version of Nate, barely visible, skimming the surface.

But there is still his phone. Left behind like a weighted thing, anchoring her to this moment. To him.

✒

Nate forgot his phone on the charger.

After soaking for nearly an hour, Claire reaches for Nate's phone, water sloughing off her skin, thin and cool. The draft chills her even more.

> I miss us. I miss you.

Two bare little sentences, too fragile to buoy her up, too whole to sink.

They leave her shipwrecked, limbs floating in the weightless void of their tension, heart a messy squall of love and loss and wanting. It is like an old and trusted letter she has already written, forgotten in the attic until it becomes a reminder, a betrayal, a promise.

Claire holds it out in front of her, away from the lapping water, unsure if it will sink her or save her. Maybe both. She hadn't meant to open it. She hadn't meant to pry. It was just there, sitting on the counter like a ghost of his oversight, a thin reflection of how he leaves her hanging, how he leaves her to fill in all the gaps herself.

She lets it sit on the edge.

Lets it be an object she doesn't care to look at.

But she cares too much, she always has.

So Claire reaches. And when her fingers graze the phone's smooth surface, it is the first connection she has felt to him in days. It feels like glass and guilt, curiosity and consequence. It is a sharp and surprising thing, a piece of him that remains when he isn't sure enough to.

She picks it up.

Water drips from her hands, droplets ricocheting off the screen. She tells herself it's just to check the time, to see how long she has let herself drown, but it is already too late for that. Claire has been submerged in this feeling for too long to know if she can come up without suffocating.

She is left behind in a bath she never asked for, without the words she needed to hear from him most. Without a lifeline, without a hope, without a sure thing. He left her with less, and now he has left her with a quiet hour and an empty promise of what used to be.

He has left her before, but this time he draws her a bath.

She pulls the phone closer, careful not to let the drops fall too heavy, too quick. Claire wants to believe that this is an oversight. That Nate forgot more than he meant to, and that he will still remember to hold onto her when she reaches.

He's the only one who ever knew where to find her heart.

And the only one who's ever lost it.

She stares at the screen, at the four-digit passcode she knows by heart. It sits there, unanswered and loyal, an untyped love letter that waits for her to fill it in. Claire hesitates, imagines herself diving in and letting it absorb. Imagines herself opening it to see what she's always known: Nothing.

But there's a note. "C"

Two fragile sentences. Two sentences that feel like an affair of the heart, a betrayal of his usual silence, the first true and gentle thing she has heard from him in days. Water drips onto the screen.

Her fingers tremble as she reads it again.

It's not what she expected.

She expects to see more distance, a silent reflection of how far apart they've drifted. Another reminder that she has reached too far, that she always wants more than he can give her. The draft chills her even more.

Instead, it feels like an old letter. The kind you write in a moment of half-forgotten heat. The kind you leave unsent for years. The kind that reminds you of how close you used to be. How little you have changed. How easily you slip back into what you should never have given up.

A thing that breaks your heart and makes you whole in the same, single read. She reads it again.

I miss us. I miss you.

Claire pulls the phone closer to her chest, away from the lapping water, away from the dangerous rise of her own, drowning pulse. She didn't expect it to have this effect. Didn't expect to float like this when she has been dragged under for weeks.

Her hair is still damp and her skin is pruned. The water is tepid now. Claire is anything but. She gasps, tugs at the air like she thought it would be thinner than it is. Tugs at the letter with the same, shivery desperation.

It is long. Longer than she expected. More than she thought she could hold at once.

Nate spills his heart in small, unsure paragraphs. Nate spills his heart. And Claire soaks it all in like she's never been so full. Like she's never been so empty, so parched, so ready to go under.

"It's not just you. It's me, too. We don't touch. We don't talk. We don't ask, because we're scared the answer will be something we can't come back from."

The paragraphs are shaky, unsure. The kind that take more than an hour to write, the kind that he leaves as a last hope, not a true thing. But it is true. It is real. It is enough to buoy her up when she thought she'd been capsized.

The words echo, rise, and fill Claire in the best, most uncertain way. They carry her further than breath, deeper than silence, further than the cool stretch of an endless bath. She slackens in the cooling water, lets herself read what Nate has written. Lets herself remember what he means to her.

Claire reads it over and over, unsteady, fragile, shipwrecked in the bittersweet squall of relief.

# Fifteen

In the dim bedroom, Claire is barely breathing. The kids are asleep, but the silence is loud, echoing with years of avoidance. She sits on the edge of the bed, knees pulled to her chest like they might hold her together. The weight of what she hasn't said clogs her throat, sticky and choking.

The room is shadowed and close, thick with baby lotion and unspoken fears. Her fingers twitch at the comforter, small half-starts before she finds the words. When she does, they fall sharp and jagged into the space between them.

"I'm not here, Nate," she says, voice barely louder than a breath. Her shoulders curl inward, a slow collapse. She keeps talking, and he listens, the truth rolling out in thin, unsteady threads.

"I keep looking in the mirror, hoping to see myself again. But I still don't know who's looking back," she says, her voice barely cracking.

She is present but unseen, and she waits for him to understand.

The room is too warm, almost suffocating. She shifts her legs down, feeling the cool touch of the hardwood floor beneath her feet. Their room, their bed, their life. The comforter feels scratchy, too hot where she grips it tightly. It matches their pillows—faded blue, so worn they barely notice them anymore. Kind of like us, she thinks, but doesn't say. She fights the urge to fill the silence with something easy, something empty. To say never mind and forget I said anything. But she can't, not this time.

"We used to be more than this," she says, eyes fixed on a dent in the wall that no one will ever bother to paint over. "You and me." Her voice wavers, each word hanging heavy between them. She swallows hard, pressing on.

"The first time I really felt it was that dream I had. Remember?" Her fingers tighten around the comforter, seeking the warmth of something familiar. "It reminded me... it reminded me I was still in here somewhere." She lets the words settle, waits for them to sting.

Nate's surprise shifts into something like understanding. She watches as his eyes change, realization crashing in. His lips part, but she talks faster, afraid to stop.

"I became someone's mom, someone's wife, but stopped being Claire. And I can't, I don't..." Her words snag on each other, tripping over themselves, desperate. Her shoulders curl as if bracing for a blow, or a hug, or something in between.

She looks away, pretending to fix the comforter where her knee has left an imprint. Her voice softens to a whisper. "I don't even know who I am anymore. I don't know who we are anymore."

He's silent, and in the silence she is sure he's leaving. Not physically, not yet, but withdrawing further into the space she's too scared to follow.

Her hands work a knot into the fabric, wondering how long it will take to come undone. "It feels like I'm disappearing," she says, pressing the heel of her hand against her eye to stop the tears. "Sometimes it feels like I'm already gone."

Nate's face tightens, pain mixed with something else she can't quite name. He opens his mouth, closes it again. She isn't sure if it's relief or heartache when he doesn't interrupt. Maybe both. Her breath is shaky, coming out in little gasps as she holds herself together.

"You used to see me. I used to see me," she says, more to herself than him. "Now I'm right here, and I don't even think you notice." She glances up, just once, catching the look on his face. It's not the blankness she's dreaded but something raw and aching.

She wants to reach out and touch him, wants to see if he's real or just a dream. But her hands stay buried in the fabric, fingers working at the knot she's made. She pulls harder, unraveling the mess, wishing everything could come undone that easily.

"I never wanted to disappear," she finishes, her voice fraying at the edges. "I just wanted to be yours."

# Sixteen

The lock clicks shut, echoing in Claire's bones. Certainty blooms where anxiety once lived. She leans against the dryer, feeling its familiar surface beneath her palms, her breath a wild thing in her chest.

A moment later, Nate is there, eyes wide with surprise and something that looks like hope. The tiny room hums around them, a charged promise in the air. She's never locked the door first, never been the one to decide, but today feels like opening a long-forgotten box. His smile is tentative, a question she wants to answer. When she guides him to the dryer's edge, producing the restraints from her pocket, his surprise is electric. He's beautiful like this—unguarded, lips parting on an exhale as she circles his wrists. "Your turn," she says, her voice both playful and commanding. His laughter fills the space between them, loosening the heavy knot that's held them apart for so long.

Claire feels a quiver in her stomach as he sits. The shift in power sends her pulse racing, the change in dynamics sharp and thrilling. She wraps the soft fabric around his wrists with slow intent, every knot a bold statement of everything she hasn't said. The previous heaviness between them melts into warmth, into something raw and open. "Claire," he says, her name rough and almost reverent on his tongue. She catches his gaze, unflinching, heavy with the weight of this moment.

He doesn't flinch as she pulls the knot tighter. She steps back to admire her work, the sight of him like this—the solid, quiet strength of him waiting for her, on display—flusters her. The way he looks at her, pupils dilated and breath unsteady, makes her feel alive, like he's breathing something essential back into her. His fingers twitch against the fabric; a small moan escapes his lips. "I didn't know you had it in you," he teases, a grin breaking his seriousness.

"I didn't either," she admits, her smile matching his, the confession lifting another invisible weight from her shoulders.

The room is small and secretive, the white noise of their bodies amplified in the tight space. She fits between his knees, leaning forward until their foreheads almost touch, and the intimacy makes her shiver. The closeness of him is dizzying, every breath shared and saturated with the anticipation that pulses like a second heartbeat. Nate's presence fills the room, fills her thoughts, and she's flooded with memories of when they first started locking the door, the uncertainty, the tentative want that unfurled into wildness. She breathes him in, his scent familiar and overwhelming.

His face is inches from hers, and the restraints shift as he strains to touch her. The fabric holds, and so does he, patient and waiting. It's her move. It's all her move. "You gonna boss me around now?" he asks, a mock seriousness in his voice, the challenge softening the edges of his consonants.

"What if I am?" Claire counters, sliding a finger up his thigh, every inch of contact a thrill, a reclamation.

Nate lets out a groan, low and surrendering. His head falls back, baring his throat, inviting her. The sight steals her breath and sends a flutter low in her belly. She laughs, a joyful sound that surprises her in its loudness. "Look at you," she whispers, unable to hide the wonder in her voice.

He lowers his head again, locking eyes, and she feels like he's reached inside and wrapped his hands around her heart. It beats wildly, a series of new confessions. That she's more than a caretaker. That she can still have this. That she can take the lead, can take him. His lips find hers—needy, soft—their moans echoing in the narrow room. They kiss like they haven't in years, no urgency except the one that wraps around them both like an unspoken promise.

Time seems to expand as Claire slips the straps of her tank top off her shoulders, feeling shy and wanton under his gaze. His eyes stay on her, watch her as if she's something precious, as if she's the only thing that matters. Her skin tingles under his attention, and when she lets the shirt fall, the intensity of his gaze sends a shiver along her spine.

"God, Claire," Nate breathes, voice thick with awe and desire.

She lets the moment linger, lets him drink in the sight of her, lets herself feel the thrill of being seen, being wanted, being here. It's overwhelming and grounding all at once. His hands flex uselessly against his bonds, and she knows he's aching to touch her, to pull her in and keep her close. Her bra joins the shirt on the floor, and the sharp intake of his breath makes her bite her lip. It makes her bolder.

"You're killing me," he says, and she can hear the smile in his voice, the disbelief.

She holds his gaze and reaches for the button of her jeans, heart pounding, not with anxiety but with certainty. His eyes track every movement, a hunger and love in them that she wants to hold onto forever. Her pants slide down her legs, pooling at her feet, and She stands before him in nothing but skin and nerve.

Nate's wrists tug at the restraints again, a noise caught between a whimper and a growl escaping him. She steps closer, the space between them evaporating. Her fingers tangle in his hair; he leans into her touch with a groan that sets her nerve endings alight. She's never felt so much.

Never felt so sure. Her other hand traces the line of his jaw, his neck, until she reaches his chest. Her touch is feather-light, and he shivers beneath it, the hardness of his body a contrast to the softness of her exploration.

The outline of his erection strains against his jeans, a sight that makes heat pool between her legs, makes her ache with the need to claim him, claim this moment. She drags her thumb over the button of his pants, teasing him, the newness of being the one in control exhilarating and terrifying. "Please," he whispers, and the word sends a thrill through her.

She unbuttons his jeans slowly, savoring the way he bites his lip, the way his chest heaves. Her hand slips beneath the fabric, and she cups him, the warmth of him making her gasp. He lets out a strangled sound, pushing into her hand, desperate and undone. She grips him tighter, marveling at how hard he is, how ready. "Is this okay?" she asks, needing to hear him say it.

His response is immediate, a groan full of need and affirmation. "Yes, god, yes."

She strokes him, gentle but firm, watching the way his eyes close, the way his lips part, the way the lines of his neck strain.

The cool metal edge of the dryer bites into her thighs, anchoring her in the moment as her body unravels. The scrape of denim against her skin is rough, grounding, a delicious contrast to the softness of his mouth.

He thrusts against her hand, a rhythm that matches the pounding in her chest. The binds on his wrists dig in as he arches into her, losing himself. The sight and the sounds of him like this unravel something deep inside, a tangled fear she hadn't realized she was holding.

He's so beautiful. She's so his.

The words leave him in a rush—jumbled desire, reverence. "Need you. Claire, I need you."

She feels the slick heat building between her thighs, a testament to how much she needs him too. She knows he's close, knows she could push him there, but she wants this to last, wants to savor every moment of having him like this, of being this. She steps back, releasing him. His eyes fly open—wild, questioning.

The cool air against her bare skin is a shock, a reminder that she's still here, still solid, still doing this. He watches her, the sudden emptiness drawing a low growl from his throat, but his eyes are full of love, full of trust. "Don't stop," he says, almost begging.

"Not stopping," she assures him, her smile wide and genuine. "Just starting."

Nate pulls against his restraints, an involuntary reaction to the slow torture of her words. She slides out of her panties, deliberately, letting him see everything, leaving nothing hidden. She's dizzy with how much she wants him, with how much she wants to make him wait, make him come undone, make him see her the way he used to. The way he always has.

And then she's in his lap, his jeans rough against her bare skin, the sensation an intoxicating contrast. Her wetness slicks the denim, proof of how much she needs him. She straddles him, rocking with a rhythm of hunger and no shame. "God, Claire," he says again, his voice cracking like he's about to break apart.

His mouth crashes into hers. She loses herself in the taste of him, in the urgency between them. His tongue meets hers, and she moans into his mouth, grinding down harder. Her nipples rub against the fabric of his shirt, sending jolts of pleasure through her, and he's moving beneath her, as much as the restraints will allow, desperate to get closer, to get deeper, to get more.

"Thought about this," she whispers, pulling back just enough to speak. "Thought about having you like this."

Her confession undoes him. He gasps her name like a plea, a prayer. She pushes harder, faster, the friction almost unbearable in its deliciousness. The pressure builds, white-hot and insistent. She's never felt so in control, so wild, so utterly unhinged. She's never felt so wanted.

His eyes squeeze shut, and he's panting, every breath an unspoken devotion. "Fuck," he says, the word a broken promise. She knows he's there, knows he's holding on by the thinnest thread.

She stops, pulling away, making him wait a second longer. His eyes snap open, and they're full of disbelief and a feral kind of awe. He sight, the power, sends her right to the edge. She moves again, an excruciating tease, her own arousal soaking the air around them.

She pushes him one more time, and it's the only push he needs. He groans, deep and guttural, a sound that makes her clench with need, a sound that makes her cry out too. She feels him come, feels the release through the rough fabric, feels him lose himself beneath her. It's hot, and it's messy, and it's perfect.

They hold there, frozen in the moment, every breath shared. Her orgasm hits seconds later, rolling through her in quiet, overwhelming waves, leaving her shaking in his lap, eyes wide, mouth open in a silent scream. She feels the wetness drip down his legs, feels it mix with his, feels it bind them together.

She collapses against him, breathless and laughing. "You," Nate says, and she knows the words that would follow even if he never spoke them. They drift on the air between them, unvoiced but so damn loud. You amaze me. You're everything. You're mine.

✒

Her fingers leave goosebumps in their wake—tiny constellations mapping a new kind of longing across his skin. Nate trembles beneath her touch, muscles taut and breathing ragged, a low hum of wanting and waiting filling the charged air.

Claire watches him carefully, deliciously undone, and it makes her bold enough to tease, bold enough to bring him to the brink only to pull away with a grin. She whispers filthy promises in his ear, savoring the hitch in his breath, the way he pushes up against her, against his bonds, against the slow torture of the rough denim on his hard cock. When the detergent topples from the shelf and bounces against his thigh, they burst into laughter, the absurdity freeing them from the confines of expectation. His release is drawn out and shuddering, and they fall against each other, breathless and laughing, hearts unraveling the last tangles of fear and finding one another, whole.

Nate looks at her with awe and disbelief, lips parted in a gasp as he strains against his binds. Claire never imagined this feeling, the rush of being the one to control and deny, the delight of watching him come undone. Her hands travel the length of his arms, feeling the heat and urgency in every shiver, the newness of their roles making her bold and unsteady in the best way. His groans are low and guttural, rising in volume as she reaches the hardness of his cock, dragging her fingers along the denim with excruciating slowness.

"Tease," he breathes, his voice strained and wrecked, sending a thrill straight through her. She can hardly believe the effect—on him, on herself. The sensation is intoxicating, his need, his helplessness, his pleasure.

"You love it," she whispers back, her words making him arch against the restraints, his eyes wild with want and disbelief. She cups him through his jeans, and he bucks against her, an unrestrained motion that nearly undoes her resolve to draw this out, to make him wait.

When she pulls away again, he lets out a sound that is half desperation, half laughter, and Claire knows she's discovered something powerful.

"Fuck, Claire," Nate says, every syllable heavy with wonder. "I'm gonna lose it."

"Not yet," she taunts, leaning in to brush her lips against his, the closeness grounding and thrilling, familiar and new. The knot in her stomach unfurls with every groan, every strain of his body. He tries to deepen the kiss, tries to push against her hand as she toys with the waistband of his jeans, and the frustration in his movements is a sweet and heady thing.

She kisses him deeply, feeling his groans vibrate through her own body, the shared want like a living thing. When she finally pulls back, the breathlessness of them makes her lightheaded, makes her feel like they're floating. "God, this is... " he starts, and she finishes the sentence for him.

"Everything," Claire says, a grin spreading wide across her face, infecting him, leaving them both laughing in gasping spurts of joy.

His voice is thick with emotion and irony. "Laundry detergent. Unconventional aphrodisiac." The dry tone nearly sends her to the floor with giggles, but she's saved by his expression—the half-smile and eyebrow lift that is the heart of him. A shared moment of mirth bounces between them like the little bottle of detergent that finally tips from the shelf, bouncing against his thigh and falling with a clatter to the floor.

The sound fills the small room, bouncing off skin, off years of tension and unsaid things. Claire bangs her elbow against the shelf, and the sharpness of the pain only heightens the unreality of the situation. Her laughter is contagious and immediate, unraveling everything they thought they were before she locked the door.

It's the playfulness of it that frees them, that sends them into a spiral of joy, the final and last barrier breaking with a giggle. Her ribs ache with the sweetness of it, with the beauty of this simple, unfettered happiness. Nate looks at her with amazement and love, with the kind of raw openness she never imagined he'd wear so freely, and she drinks it in, her own happiness flooding her, filling her.

She kisses him again, long and slow, every inch of his body a promise she means to keep. Her fingers trace his lips, his throat, the outline of his shoulders, the hard lines of his chest. She pulls back to catch her breath and marvel at him, the restraint freeing him of everything but this moment, everything but her.

The intimacy of it, the vulnerability of him, is unlike anything she's ever experienced. Unlike anything she thought possible. Her hands find the bottom of his shirt, and she pulls it over his head, the sudden expanse of bare skin a revelation, a feast she wants to savor and devour. Her tongue flicks over his collarbone, tasting the salt of his effort, of his submission. "Oh god," he says, the words less and more than words.

He arches towards her again, eyes wild, muscles flexing and unflexing. "Claire. You're gonna kill me."

She's struck by how young he looks, how like the boy she fell for before they ever locked any door, and it spurs her on, makes her greedy and soft and wild. "But what a way to go," she says, catching his earlobe between her teeth and drawing another groan from him, making him jerk upwards, searching for her with his body.

He strains against the soft bindings again, against the intimacy of her voice, of her nearness. Her hands move to the button of his jeans, slowly unfastening it, the teasing making them both breathless with anticipation. He lets out a sound, more animal than human, when she finally slips her hand inside, when she finally gives him the smallest taste of what he wants. "Oh fuck, Claire."

She strokes him through his boxers—gentle, deliberate—the softness both promise and challenge. She lets the boxers slip down, watching his cock spring free, hard and slick and so fucking beautiful.

Her confidence swells, new and thrilling and shared, the reflection of it in his eyes making her wetter, making her bolder, making her need this more than she needs air. She grips him tighter, and his head falls back, his cries unrestrained and full of awe.

He trembles under her touch, under the exquisite torture of her control, under the weightlessness of surrender. The binds around his wrists leave faint marks, small and temporary and claiming. “Please,” he says, and his vulnerability leaves her gasping, leaves her undone.

“Yes,” she breathes, and she knows it’s all she needs to say.

She works him harder, faster, each motion bringing him closer, bringing him right to the edge. He moans, a long, drawn-out sound that fills the air, that fills her ears, that fills her whole world with the surety of him. With the surety of them. His cock strains against her fist, impossibly hard, impossibly needy, and she lets out a sound of her own, a keening whimper as his urgency becomes her own.

“Need to see you,” he gasps, and the demand is more giving than taking.

His words undo her. His everything undoes her. Her free hand slips between her legs, finding herself soaked, finding herself ready, finding herself lost in how much she wants this, how much she wants him. He watches her through heavy-lidded eyes, and the intensity makes her want to come without ever being touched. Her fingers work her clit with a ferocity that matches the strokes on his cock, and she’s falling, falling, falling with the promise of it.

The restraints bite into him again, and it’s too much, and she knows it, knows it like she’s never known anything, knows it like the way his hips jerk up to meet her, like the way his eyes screw shut, like the way he calls out her name as he comes in shuddering, wet, exquisite pulses that she watches, that she feels, that she takes as a part of him she will never give back.

The force of it makes him dizzy, leaves him breathless and open, a picture of beautiful surrender. Claire, heaving with want, rubs herself faster, harder, frantic, wet, relentless. She pushes herself over the edge, her own release following seconds later, a crashing, silent scream that fills the room, fills her mind, fills the spaces in her heart that used to feel like fear.

His come glistens across his belly, his cock still straining against her hold as she collapses forward, letting go, her arms finding his neck, her body finding his, her spirit finding the most important parts of her she never thought she'd find again.

She unties his wrists, hands tender and unsure as she does. The ropes leave impressions that will disappear. He pulls her in, soft and spent, holding her close, their skin damp and sticking together, the intimacy breathtaking.

His voice is as low and rough as it's ever been. "Hey, Claire."

She shifts to look at him, and the satisfaction in his eyes leaves her speechless.

"Your turn," Nate says, smiling, the suggestion playful and serious and everything at once.

Claire leans in, lips grazing his ear. "Then watch me," she whispers.

# Seventeen

The black silk slips through Nate's calloused fingers, cool as river water against the heat building under Claire's skin. She can't see him yet, but she can hear his slow, sure steps across the floor. Can feel her heart beating through every nerve. Can imagine how it will be—blind, bound, her whole body one desperate pulse. Nate holds the blindfold out, waits for her small nod before wrapping it snug, plunging her into a darkness that makes her ache.

Claire is a tangle of need and nerves. Already spread on the bed, the room dim and hushed around her. She waits, hears Nate coming closer. Her heart drums wild beneath each breath. She feels each sound as if it were a touch—his movements deliberate, unhurried, impossible to resist. She remembers the first time they locked the door. The first time she couldn't keep quiet, couldn't keep her grip on reality. She is unraveling again, and the need is almost feral. Almost too much.

His presence fills the room, all slow certainty and intention. She doesn't have to see him to know he's close. Doesn't need sight to tremble with want. The blindfold is still in his hands, black against his skin, and Claire feels the image burn behind her eyes. Already she's imagining losing herself in him, how it will feel when the world reduces to breath, to touch, to him. The need swells and aches, a tightness in her chest, her voice.

He brings the blindfold to her, one slow hand caressing her hair, the other raising the silk over her eyes. It slides against her temples, smooth and light, but the effect is instant. Binding. She lets out a soft, shivery gasp as Nate ties it in place. Her world narrows to a single desperate point, sight disappearing, leaving only the echo of his touch and her heartbeat thudding inside her. She's blind now. Soon she'll be bound. Soon he'll push her so far she won't know where she begins and he ends.

Darkness washes over her in deep waves. Nate's breath is closer now, ragged and wanting against her neck. He touches her shoulders, leans in with a whisper that sends fire down her spine. "Beautiful," he murmurs. "Spread out for me like this. So perfect, Claire." The heat of him is unbearable. The words break her open. She's trembling before he even begins. "My girl," he says, voice low and reverent. "You know what I'll do to you."

He guides her, helps her fall back, the mattress shifting under his weight as he moves. Her pulse is everywhere, quick and sharp. She imagines herself as he sees her: legs bent, hair spilling around her, lips parted and breathing his name. The scent of him fills her lungs. His cologne, the familiar and heady mix of skin and soap and Nate. She gives in to it, to him, lets out a small, shaking sound as she arches, searching blindly for more. Her cheeks are flushed, her body pulling toward his, toward the promise she knows he'll keep.

She remembers how he tied her hands at the mirror, how he made her watch every unfiltered second. The way her voice broke when she came, when she begged. The way his body felt, sure and hard against her back. "Don't look away," he had whispered, and she couldn't. She didn't want to. Not when he touched her like that. Not when he touched her like he knew she would break apart and trusted him to keep her whole. She knows he'll push her to the edge again tonight. Her body, already reacting, needs this. Needs him.

Every moment that passes makes her shiver more, her anticipation bleeding into panic, into urgency. The blindfold clings damp to her skin. Her heart is so loud, so fast. Nate's weight on the bed shifts again, a long exhale. She imagines his eyes on her, how dark they get when he watches her come undone. How much she wants them, even though she can't see. A whimper slips through her teeth. Nate pins her wrists. She pulls against him, but he keeps her there, strong and steady. She is shaking now, barely able to breathe, unable to be without this another second.

"Nate, please," she gasps, and his low hum nearly unravels her. His hands slide down her arms, firm, deliberate. It makes her body jerk and seize. He keeps her pinned with only his grip and his voice, his slow words an anchor. "That's it, baby," he says. "Give me everything." His voice is so sure, so close. "You know I'll take it." She doesn't answer; she doesn't have to. He can feel how hard her pulse is through her skin. She wants this. She needs this.

He lets her wrists go and drags his hand down, down. She is velvet and fire, exposed and aching and ready. "You love this, don't you?" he asks, already knowing, his breath hot against her cheek. She is strung so tight she can't even answer, just nods against him and pushes up, as much as she can, straining for his touch. Her cheeks burn, her body burns, the cool air like ice as she shivers. Nate kisses her temple. It is tender and rough all at once. It is everything she needs.

Her back arches with the want of it, her hips rising off the bed. A long, broken sound escapes her lips. He runs his fingertip down her center, a trail of fire that makes her jerk. She is wet and already undone, his light touch like lightning. The mattress shifts again. She breathes him in, tastes how close he is, how thick the want is in her throat. His lips brush the shell of her ear, and she's so lost she doesn't know if she can be found. Not yet. Not unless he brings her back.

His hands weave into her hair, holding her, pulling her in as he works his way down her neck with his mouth. A soft, low noise gets caught in her throat, but Nate swallows it with a kiss that makes her knees draw up, makes her muscles quake against the mattress. He pulls away and moves down, his breath a whisper against her stomach. The warmth and weight of him is almost too much. The way her body betrays her, trembling and exposed, is almost more than she can bear. Her breath catches, and she's already begging. She needs him, needs all of it.

Nate is her world, the single, crashing point of it, and she feels herself falling hard. Her body is a tremor that he's already set off, shaking and relentless and his.

✒

The bindings are silk against her wrists. Nate pulls them snug, not tight enough to hurt but tight enough to remind her who she belongs to. Tight enough that she can't do anything but feel.

Claire lets out a shivering breath, and Nate kisses her there, keeps his lips pressed to her pulse as it flutters beneath the skin. He ties the other wrist, then pulls back to admire his work, murmuring how proud he is, how much he's going to give her.

She is exposed and breathless, each word making her shudder more. Her mind is already hazy, spinning, and his voice is the only thing grounding her. The silk feels different now that she can't see it. It feels like everything is new, shocking and overwhelming in the most perfect way. "Beautiful," he whispers, rough fingertips working. "Look how needy you are for me." He binds her left wrist the same way, ties the knot slow and sure. His touch feels so heavy she almost breaks.

She gasps for air as he pulls away, moves down her body with the same deliberate attention, the same possessive grip. Every motion is charged, electric. She imagines the way his eyes burn into her, and she almost wishes she could see. Almost. She pulls against the ties, muscles trembling, body arching into every fiber. She has no idea where the darkness ends and he begins. Only that she belongs to him. That he'll keep her from falling apart too soon.

He gathers both arms in one strong hand, stretches her above her head like a gift. Like she's his and only his. Claire lets out a whimper that he catches with his mouth, swallowing it before it gets too loud. The bed shifts beneath her as he leans in, as his weight presses down. She shivers and holds her breath and holds nothing else. Her thighs are already damp, but she knows he won't let her break— not yet. Not until she's so close she forgets which way is down.

He fastens her to the bedposts, one hand gripping her arm, one working the ties with calm precision. He knows what this does to her, how helpless it makes her feel. How safe it makes her feel. He knows that every time he does it, she needs it more. She trembles as he checks each restraint, making sure they'll hold, making sure she knows who owns every shiver. Her breath catches, and her world spirals, contracts, all darkness and anticipation.

"You want more, Claire?" Nate's voice is deep and low, like a spark that sets off every nerve in her body. He runs his thumb down the length of her arm, a soft trail that makes her writhe. She pushes up, desperate, urgent, too breathless to answer. Too sure of his strength, of his hold, to care. "Can't see, can't move. You're perfect," he says, and she strains for him. For the warmth and weight she knows is so close.

Her breath is shallow and sharp as he moves down, his touch light as air, burning like fire. Claire lets out a hard exhale, and her voice gets caught on the want of it, on how close she is to losing control. She pulls again and again, tries to escape just so he can hold her tighter. So he can tell her how much he loves it when she fights and falls apart and trusts him to pick up every piece. Her heart beats too fast, her pulse a white-hot drum, and still he doesn't let her go.

He takes his time undressing her, takes his time watching her shiver. Each second is a crackle of electricity, a raw intake of air. He holds her down with his stare, with the power of his focus and hands and voice. With the weight of his wanting. She fights it, loves it, needs it. Nate kisses her shoulder, then moves lower. The heat of him is more than she can bear, and a moan slips from her lips, unbidden and uncontrolled. It undoes him.

His mouth is a whisper against her, all praise and promise. She is already spread and needy and wild. The way he moves is so sure, so steady, that Claire doesn't know how she'll make it to the end without breaking first. "Look at you, baby. Can't get enough, can you?" He kisses her hips, and she gasps, tries to draw him in with her legs, with her silence and pleading and will. But he knows, and she knows, and still he takes his time. Still he takes everything.

The mattress shifts beneath her as he moves, as his hands slide lower, pulling at the elastic of her yoga pants. It feels like a jolt, like a rush of cold and need and want. His breath is warm on her stomach, his hands confident and slow, and she is shaking already. She is wanting too much. He lets his fingers trail down her center, light, so light, but enough to make her thrash against him. Her whole body moves, all frantic desperation, and she's too far gone to hold back, too lost to even care.

"Just you and me, Claire. Just us." His voice is a low, growling thing, full of promise, full of power. The feel of it sends a shudder up her spine, makes her arch into the nothingness, into the black, and beg. Nate presses his mouth to her again, his beard scratching her soft skin, her thigh, the most sensitive parts of her. She is slick and pliant, raw and wet, the pulse between her legs a match for the one in her throat, her wrists, her chest. She pushes her hips up and up, losing herself to the urgency. "You need more?"

Her answer is a cry, a gasp, a shivering mess. It doesn't matter. Nate hears it all.

He goes slow, steady, so sure of his strength and the effect it has on her, so sure that she'll give in before he ever does. He loves that, too. The scent of him floods her senses, the heat and skin and heavy want, and Claire is pulled in deeper. Deeper and drowning. She breathes him in, loses herself to the hard push of his calloused hands, the softness of his lips, the way he kisses every inch and keeps her waiting, keeps her begging. He works his way down, doesn't let up, doesn't let her slip. Not yet.

Her legs are bent and slick against him, her breathing sharp and strained and as ragged as it's ever been. She doesn't know what she's asking for. She doesn't care. She just knows she needs it, all of it, and she needs it now.

✒

She doesn't need to see to know what he's doing. The hum of the drawer is the only sound in the room, and Claire is already wet, already shaking as he brings the plug to her skin. It feels impossibly big as he works it in, as it stretches her with relentless patience. Her cry is a shuddering, undone thing, and Nate comes unraveled.

Claire's heart beats with the hum, frantic and too fast. She can barely catch her breath. Nate moves with calm deliberation, taking his time, knowing how wild it makes her. Her voice is a mess already, a small, aching thing as she pulls against the restraints. He watches her tremble, hears the frantic urgency of her need. “Last time was just a taste,” he says, and the words make her whole body tense, arch, strain for him. Remembers the mirror, how exposed she felt. How perfect it was. She is already gone, and he hasn’t even touched her.

He doesn’t have to. Her pulse quickens with the sound of the drawer, with the promise of what she knows he’s going to do. Her muscles are a sharp, pulsing tremor. She knows how this ends. She can’t wait. Nate is close enough for her to feel the heat of him, close enough for her to know she’ll be begging soon. A rough exhale escapes her, desperate and sharp.

His hands are on the plug, warming it. His voice is low, like gravel, like thunder, as he tells her what’s next. She fights to stay grounded, but it’s impossible with his weight on the bed, the heat of him between her legs. His skin is so close she can taste it. Her body jerks and quakes, and her words are a mangled sound. Her voice is an open thing, and he loves that too.

“Ready, Claire?” he asks, and the first touch makes her shake. The first touch makes her whole body buck. He is impossibly patient, the opposite of how she feels. He strokes her stomach, then moves lower. Lower. She lets out a frantic, broken cry, and he shushes her, soothes her with strong hands, with soft strokes, with everything she needs. Her pulse is ragged and frantic, a blur of red-hot want. His sure movements make it burn even brighter. Her anticipation becomes fire, becomes ache. Becomes now.

He presses the plug against her, lubed and cold, the promise of more. The promise of everything. Her muscles tighten around it, and her whole world dissolves. Each push stretches her further, deeper, until she’s not sure she can take anymore, until she’s not sure she can survive if he stops. Claire pulls hard against the restraints. He sees her, loves her, knows how close she is to snapping.

He loves that.

She is burning up, every nerve alive and begging. Her body is one frantic beat, a want so big she can't contain it. The stretch and fullness make her writhe, make her mindless. She can't see. She can't move. Her legs are already wet against him, a glistening, needful thing. Nate activates the vibration and holds her as she cries out, watches her arch, makes sure she can't come unhinged without him. She is teetering, right there, ready to fall apart. And he knows it.

The vibrations are so deep she can barely breathe. Her whole body moves with them, and her voice is all shuddering noise. She fights for more, pushes for more, is more. She has lost track of herself, of him, of the everything. She just knows she needs it to end. She needs it to never end. Her pulse is a live wire, her breath one long quake. Nate gives her just enough, tells her she's beautiful, that he's not done with her yet. The words send her spinning, send her reeling. Her body can't take it anymore. Her mind is a frenzy of moans, a soft chant of begging, of wanting, of Nate.

He knows that too.

She is soaked and aching, every part of her one bright heat. He holds her steady as she falls apart, gives her the edge, holds her just far enough back. "This?" he says, touching the plug. "Or this?" pressing it in. Her cry is the answer he wants, the answer she needs to give. Her hips lift in the most desperate arc, the vibration pulsing against the frantic thud of her heart. He takes it lower, then even lower, and she lets out a wail that's almost a sob.

"Please, Nate," she gasps, and it comes out a tremor. Comes out a raw, wrecked plea. "Please, I need—"

She doesn't get to finish. He knows what she needs.

She is so lost she might not make it back. Her mind and body spiral, urgent and heady, so far gone she can't be found. Not until he fills her. Not until he takes it. He releases the tie on her wrist just long enough to pull her legs wider, just long enough to remind her what it's like to touch, to feel. Then he's in between, in her, and the slick stretch of him is so much she can't breathe. Can't do anything but lose herself. The vibration makes her convulse. The fullness makes her whole. He presses her legs to her chest, tells her to take it all, and she comes undone at the rough, perfect sound of his voice.

He is her whole world, and he pushes in harder, deeper, in time with the plug, in time with the relentless wanting. Her voice cracks, and she is too far gone to hold it together. Too far gone to care. His pace quickens, and he feels impossibly big, feels so perfect that she doesn't know how to keep from shattering. She doesn't know how to keep breathing. She pulls against the restraints, too wild to stop, her legs shaking as he drives into her.

Nate watches her fall apart, takes her deeper, faster, loves her harder than he ever has. The stretch and the vibration and the force of him make her mindless. Make her his. She is crying now, gasping, too lost to know where she begins and ends. "Let go, Claire," he says, and her world turns white-hot, turns heat and light and too much and more.

She breaks apart with his name, and he keeps her steady. Her body shakes with the release, her words sharp and choked and overwhelming. "Good girl," he murmurs, never slowing, never letting her slip. Her voice is ragged, breathless, and he loves it. Loves the way she opens up, the way she takes it for him. "Don't stop, Claire. Take it all."

It's more than she can hold, but he doesn't stop.

She is a shivering mess. Her whole world a blissful, brutal blur. Her muscles clench around the plug, around him. She is an endless pulse of breaking, of becoming, of raw release. She doesn't hold back. She doesn't try. She doesn't have to. Her words are lost to the swell of it all, to the crash of feeling, to the wreck and rebuild and relentless pounding.

The silk at her wrist shifts with each pull—soft, warm, just enough to remind her she's real, she's held, she's here.

She sobs against him, and he pushes deeper, harder, faster. "You're so beautiful like this," he says. "I love watching you come."

Her whole body arches, then crumbles. Her words a low, broken wail. "Nate, I'm—"

"Yes," he says, giving her everything. "Again, baby. Let go." Her back lifts, her world dissolves, and she is shuddering and raw. She's coming. Again.

And then again.

He pushes deeper, harder, until the world blurs at the edges and she is nothing but breath and release and a long, wild pulse. Her cries are almost sobs. Her begging is just the beginning.

Claire shakes uncontrollably as Nate keeps up the same hard, urgent rhythm. Her voice is frantic and broken as she calls his name, as she gives him everything. He pounds into her with no intention of stopping, no intention of letting up. His force is unrelenting, a drive that she can't resist. A drive that he loves.

She's coming so hard she might split in two, but Nate's voice keeps her whole. "Again, Claire. You're so beautiful like this." Her words are strangled and thick, an uneven rush of sound, but still she gives them. Her body is beyond breaking, beyond release. Her muscles clench tight around him, tighter, so tight she doesn't know if she can take more. But she does. He makes sure she does.

"Take it," he says, low and demanding, in time with each forceful thrust, in time with the wreckage he's making of her body and breath. Her heart beats out of her chest, out of her throat, her pulse fast and hard, relentless, and he's the same. Her back arches as another climax slams through her. Her legs are slick against his chest, against her skin, against the world that dissolves into heat and blur. She is breaking apart. She is barely holding together.

"Please," she cries, "please, Nate, I—" But the words vanish. Her mind vanishes. She trembles in his grasp, limbs limp and humming with aftershock. "Oh god, oh god," she gasps, the vibration still working her from the inside. "Oh god, I can't—" But she can. And she does.

Her begging is raw, a noise of impossible desperation. He knows how to push her. Knows how to make her break and love it. She has no words now, only high, keening sounds, and it doesn't matter. Nate knows what they mean. His voice is even and steady, a rock against her frenzy. "You're not done," he says, and she knows she's not. Not until he lets her. Not until he's taken every last piece. "Take it for me," he says, and her release is wild, a furious, throbbing heat. "Don't stop."

She doesn't know if she'll survive. Isn't sure she cares. She's his, all his, her body and her will and her voice that gives everything, every time. "You want this, don't you?" he says, and she sobs as another wave hits, as another spiral makes her tremble from her bones to her skin. Her voice is jagged and lost, a call, an echo. Her body responds, gives it back to him, wraps around him in one final, helpless plea.

She is weightless. She is a live wire. She is a tethered spark, a burst of endless sensation. And still he doesn't let up. Still he doesn't stop. "Oh god, I'm—" she gasps, but she's not even sure where she is, not even sure if she's really still there. His presence is so deep, so complete, that she's almost convinced he's everywhere. His body. His words. His insistence. It's too much. It's everything.

He knows. He wants it that way. He holds her tight, relentless, making her take all of him, making her need more. He is a furious, perfect heat. He is the world closing in. She doesn't want it to stop.

She feels it too. Feels all of it. The plug is a constant, a deep thrum that keeps her suspended, a stretch and vibration that doesn't stop. Not even when she does. Not even when she can't. Nate moves in time with it, in time with her frantic pulse. She is slick skin and wild abandon, caught in a rhythm with no end. She's coming in gasps, in shudders, in a long, chaotic chant of his name. "Yes," he says, feeling her unravel. "Keep going." His words push her over, send her reeling. Her muscles give, then take, then give again, and it's all for him.

The pleasure borders on pain, and still it grows, a relentless rise that makes her voice thin, sharp, so full that she might be empty. So full she might explode. She pulls against the restraints with surprising force, a wildness that breaks everything, especially herself. Especially the last bit of control. The mattress is damp with the mess she's made, with her release, and still Nate gives more, still he takes more. "You can do this," he says, pulling her hips in tighter.

She wants to. She will.

Her body is lost, completely shattered. She doesn't know how much longer she can last, how much longer she can hold on, but she gives him everything. She trusts him with everything. Her body is wrecked, but Nate never stops, never lets her slip, not even when her mind does. Not even when the last thread of sense snaps. His voice is everywhere, more than her pulse, more than the impossible stretch, more than she can believe. More than her. "Nate, I'm—" But she isn't sure. Isn't sure what, isn't sure where. She's too far gone, her voice a hitching sob, her words a desperate release, her whole body so fragile she might not make it back. She's shattered beyond any limit she's ever known. "Nate, I'm—"

Her world dissolves into white noise—static and soundless.

He guides her through it, never slowing, never stopping.

He loves her through it, deep and raw.

He makes her do the same.

He kisses her damp cheek, cradles her like she's new. Like he can hold every piece, and he will. Like he's not the only one. He is still inside her, deep and sure and hers, and she feels herself become.

He wraps his arms around her, steady and safe, keeps her tight and loved and his. He holds her like this, like everything, lets her breathing slow, lets her world slow. Her heart beats against his chest. He is all she knows. She is raw, a bright thread of feeling. He lets her become. She sags into him, lets him hold it all.

"Good girl," he whispers. Her pulse is a dull, pounding thud, but it starts to even out. The static noise of release turns quiet, but not silent. Not with him. He loves her through the fragility, loves her through the calm. Loves her as the chaos gives way to bliss, to connection, to love. Her voice is a soft, muted echo, and he keeps her grounded, keeps her warm and known.

Claire lets out a slow, hitching breath. Lets him take it, take her, stay deep inside her as she unravels. Her body shudders through the aftershocks, but he stays—steady, sure, hers. His pace is slow, so slow, a whisper of what it was, but just as powerful. Just as much. Just enough. He stays with her through it, lets her come back, lets her build up from the break.

Her hands are weak, her limbs shaking, and he is her whole world. She loves the feel of him, the stretch of him, the deep, persistent knowing. Her skin is damp and sticky, and he loves her through that too. He tells her as much with every lingering push. He holds her with every beat. He holds her tight as the last tremor shakes through, as her breath turns rough and new. He is all of it, all she needs.

Nate doesn't pull out. He doesn't pull back. He presses closer, his body anchoring her fragile self, his voice holding her whole. "My girl," he says, and she is, always. She trembles at the words, warms to the weight of them, feels them deeper than anything else. She is overwhelmed and delicate, a flood of raw feeling, and Nate is everything that keeps her steady.

Her skin burns where he touches her, and she arches to him, pushes into him, opens for him all over again. The light is dim and soft, and she starts to adjust, to see him, to see how completely he's filled her world. How much he still is. His hands are so gentle, so tender, so unlike the way she's felt, and it makes her want him more.

He releases her from the restraints, strokes the silk over her wrists like a memory, like a promise. He moves with the same care he always does, with the same love. He works the ties slowly, patiently, tells her not to rush, tells her he's right there. She's never heard words so beautiful.

Nate is everywhere, his touch, his voice, his breath, and she surrenders to it, to him, lets herself go again. He massages her hands, keeps the warmth in them, keeps the life in them. She's not sure how he manages to hold so much, but he does, and she's grateful, and she's his. She gives in to him like the softest breath.

The blanket is a gentle weight around her, a sure weight that wraps her up, but Nate is even more so. He's her blanket. Her warmth. Her everything. She feels him cover her, feels him swallow her whole, and she never wants it to stop. Not when he makes her this safe. This wanted. This loved.

He kisses her lips, lets the salt of her sweat and the wetness of her mouth blend with his own, lets her breathe it in, breathe him in, fill her lungs and chest and soul with only him. Her body goes slack and easy, and he's the reason. Her body is the happiest it's ever been, and Nate's still there. Still moving.

She's trembling in the softest, most sacred way, and he knows how to take it. He knows just how to love it. He removes the plug last, careful and slow, holds her through it, holds her as the wet mess of it makes her sigh, makes her draw him in and trust him with everything. “So proud of you,” he says, and it’s the most perfect sound she’s ever heard. “So proud.”

His words flood her, fill her to the brim, a quiet intensity making her gasp, a low vibration spreading from her heart to her limbs. She lets it carry her. Lets it take her somewhere safe, warm, whole. She is cradled in it, in him, and the world can’t touch her here. Only Nate can.

He’s so soft, so gentle, so full of love that she can barely believe it, but she does. She does.

The mattress is damp with sweat and trust, and Nate doesn’t mind. He wraps her in his arms, cradles her as if he’s holding everything. Claire trembles against him, overflowing with something so deep it feels holy.

‘I love you,’ he says.

And she cries because it’s true.

# Epilogue

Claire enters the house, closing the door softly behind her. No clatter of toys or syrupy squeals. Just the muted buzz of the dryer vibrating through the walls, so soft she barely hears it over the quiet pound of her pulse.

With the kids at her mother's, she should start the dishwasher or maybe clear out the crumbled Goldfish from the couch cushions, but all she does is stand, a little dazed by the rarity of it—this quiet that echoes, wide and uninterrupted. A smile curls across her lips, sly and slow. She moves through the hall, each step slow, deliberate, fingers trailing the wall like she's just remembered it's there. She pauses at the laundry room, the air a little warmer, a little more electric, and steps inside, Watching the slow, steady thrum of the dryer. The room is just big enough for reckless decisions, and she knows every inch of it by heart. She folds the laundry basket onto the counter, breath deepening as she reaches for the door. She closes it with a soft but decisive click. The lock sounds like a promise in the quiet. When she turns around, he's already there, leaning against the dryer with a look that says he's exactly where he's meant to be.

The house holds its breath, the quiet even more poignant with him there. Nate doesn't say anything, just looks at her with eyes that understand every layer of her—the wife, the mother, the woman she's letting herself become again. His presence fills the room, but she feels the expanse of it between them, charged and vibrating. The dryer hums along, a domestic thrum that anchors and elevates them at once. His lips curl in a knowing smile, broad and slow, making her pulse race with everything unspoken between them. It was always like this in here, first frantic, then sweetly desperate, and now—a different kind of intimacy, every bit as consuming.

Claire's smile matches his as she crosses the room, the act so deliberate it borders on teasing. She feels wild with how easy it is to want like this. Just them. Just now. Just exactly what it should be. Her heart kicks in her chest as she leans against the counter, the warmth of the dryer in her skin and in her bones. His eyes stay locked on hers, and she sees the silent way it undoes him, that she's the one who locked the door this time. The memory of their first reconnection unfurls between them, intimate and charged—a shaky experiment that led to a promise. That led to this. Her breath is shallow but sure. Her fingers curl around the edge of the counter.

The quiet and closeness cocoon them, blurring everything else to softness. He watches her, eyes steady as gravity, like he'll wait forever to see what she does next. She sees his breath deepen, chest moving under that old grey shirt, and she thinks about all the times he caught her in the stairwell, the garage, against a wall, against this dryer. She knows how to move. She knows how this ends. And with him watching like that—intent and unhurried, anticipation drawing out the space between them—she also knows how to make it last.

They face each other in the tight space, the quiet louder than any chaos, all breaths and locked glances and the metallic rumble of the dryer.

It should be overwhelming—the urgency, the intimacy, the fucking perfect way he watches her. She's barely taken a breath before he's on her, pulling her in with hands that should be frantic but aren't, should be rushed but aren't.

Somehow, he makes a fast, sharp intake of breath last forever. It's the way he is, the way they are—unhurried in their reckless hunger, reverent in their dirty devotion. His fingers hook in the straps of her tank top, the hem of his shirt. Their silence is its own dirty language, a pulse they learned to speak again after the madness of three kids, of too little sleep and too many unspoken fears. The tank slides down her arms; the shirt comes up over his shoulders. Her back meets the dryer, and the vibrations roll through her spine, everything a little too loud, a little too sharp, a little too fucking much in the best way. He's holding her hips, holding her gaze, moving deep and thick and completely hers.

He draws her to him, skin on skin, the slow burn of their touch like wildfire. Claire's breath hitches as he wraps her in his arms, the steadiness of his hold a promise she feels everywhere. Her fingers trace the hem of his jeans, an unspoken need, before he moves—deft, intentional—guiding her legs around him, lifting her with ease, her world narrowing to this. Her eyes close, a soft moan escaping, before he lets her settle back on the dryer. She's there, half-wrecked and half-aching to be wrecked more, every inch of her tuned to the way he watches her, the way he handles her, like she's a treasure he's kept for himself. The world spins, hot and dizzy, when his mouth finds hers again, deep and searching and possessive. She arches into him, a sound of pure want rumbling from her chest.

His fingers brush her thigh, a teasing trail up the line of her leg to where he needs her. Her pulse thrums beneath her skin, wild and free, as his hand traces the curve of her ass. Then, her shorts are gone, and she is all slick heat beneath his calloused hands. The way he explores her—fingers coaxing and insistent—undoes every last bit of hesitation she has, every last doubt. The dryer vibrates beneath her, hot with the threat of everything. She can barely breathe for how fucking alive it makes her feel.

He groans, low and filthy and grateful, when she pulls him against her, urgent and insistent. His jeans hang loose around his hips, and he kicks them away, their breath colliding and mingling. The moment holds, sharp and wanting, as his cock grinds against her, then moves with a familiar, beautiful rhythm. Claire gasps, wild and wanting, his name on her lips as he thrusts deep, pushing her back into the warmth of the dryer. Each movement hums through her, his skin against hers, her heartbeat syncing with the snap of his hips. She is all instinct and reckless abandon, caught up in how easily he fills her, the dirty slide of his body as her legs tighten around his waist.

Nate braces against the wall with one hand, his forehead pressed to hers, breaths sharp and clipped, her pulse racing in tandem with his. Claire clutches at his shoulders, lost in the rough and tender way he takes her. Her back arches, her spine curves, The friction and closeness consume her as her hands slip to his hips, urging him deeper, again and again. The room feels smaller, hotter, and impossibly vast, each thrust carrying the weight of everything they've fought to keep. The look on his face, the intensity of it, the desperation of it, unravels her. She clings to him, body taut, a tight-wire of need and sweet release as she breaks, as she shatters, as the pressure explodes. He takes her through it, slowing the roll of his hips as her muscles quake and quiver around him, gasping breaths against his mouth, and then follows, his quiet groan cutting through the air. The world fades out, spiraling, tightening, until it's only them, only this, only the hum and heat and fucking heaven of having each other.

The air is heavy with their breaths, with the weight of everything, with the beautiful nothing of being just them. Nate leans back, and they both laugh, hushed and disbelieving, breathless in their tangled wonder. The sound is relief, not humor. Joy, not surprise. She presses her face to his neck, body melting into his as they stay locked together. They breathe in sync, in waves, each exhale a reminder of how perfectly they fit.

He shifts, voice rough but playful. "Don't forget to switch it to delicate," he murmurs. She laughs again, dizzy with how happy she is. "Too late," she says, lips brushing his. Nate lifts her off the dryer, cradles her against him, carries her to their unmade bed. This time, she knows exactly where they're meant to be.

The screen lights up. Caps. Gifs. Chaos. Claire scrolls to the latest messages, already laughing. This is what they do best: confess too much, delete later, love each other through the mess. There's a fresh message waiting — from Brielle, of course.

Don't Read This Aloud, Karen
Sat, Mar 13 at 8:04 PM

Brielle

is it weird to want
something…

that you're pretty sure your
partner would say yes to

but only if they thought it
wasn't real

Naomi

context, please

Claire

what are you trying to do

Brielle

something I probably
shouldn't want

but I do

Rachel

if this ends with a babysitter
fantasy i'm logging off

Brielle

A second opinion...?

Claire

brielle wtf

Harper

wait WHAT

ma'am?!

Naomi

...elaborate immediately

Claire giggles, imagining her red-haired calm in contrast to the dramatic thread. Queen Naomi, a little older than the rest of them, but infinitely wiser. Claire bets she would have a perfect plan for it all. An actual spreadsheet. The idea makes her grin. Naomi probably predicted this months ago, right down to the trash fire of messages it would ignite.

Her thighs still ache.

Her body still hums.

Nate's touch hasn't faded.

Her phone vibrates again.

Naomi

don't hold out.

who's the new boy toy?

Claire almost drops the phone.

She sets it down.

Breathes.

Remembers.

The heat.

The stretch.

The lock on the laundry room door.

She picks the phone back up.

Claire

more like an old toy

and it's fucking AMAZING

Brielle

NO U DID NOT

bitch what the actual fck

Claire knows exactly what her voice would sound like, what all of them sound like, and it makes her laugh, loud and a little unhinged, because this is who they are. The real housewives of Karen, their lives messy and wild, confession flying fast enough to make her dizzy.

She's learned to love it, to need it, this shared chaos with her mom club co-conspirators. She wonders what they'd say if she confessed everything, absolutely everything, how far they've taken it all, how far they're planning to go. If they'd believe any of it.

Her cheeks are flushed as she starts to type again.

Claire

hypothetically

Rachel

DELETE THIS

like. literally delete.

i'm sweating

Harper

so is a little competition
gonna help or hurt

because omg I have IDEAS

Naomi

well.

are you gonna let her win?

A gif drops.

Simone Biles lands a vault with flawless smugness. Claire cackles. She feels seen. Lit up. Free. She types for a while, hesitating to hit send before someone has clearly seen those flickering ellipsis dots hovering for way too long. Another message pops in.

Harper

send it

Claire stares at the words, at her reflection in the dark screen.

She doesn't know if Harper means the text, the scandal, or the whole secret life she's starting to love.

But maybe, finally… she's ready to send it all.

# Nate

He finds the plug at the bottom of the box, under picture frames and old concert tees and a life that once felt reckless and brave. It's been months since they first locked that door. It's smaller than Nate remembers, a hard jewel against his palm, and His thumb skims the smooth edge, like he's relearning her body by muscle memory alone.

It's the kind of toy that used to make Claire blush and gasp, even after she got brave enough to wear it under a slinky black dress. He almost can't believe she kept it—buried under years of exhaustion and the kind of roommate marriage they promised they'd never have. He wants to take it downstairs, show it to her, ask her who she is now that the kids are away for the weekend and the house is quiet. He wants to tell her about the other box—the one she doesn't know he found—and ask if she's ready to open it too.

He turns the plug over, lets it rest heavy in his hand. They haven't used it in years, but he still remembers her trembling beneath him, her body open and hungry, her skin burning under his touch. He remembers her begging for more, his own pulse wild with the thrill of watching her take everything he could give. They didn't just have sex back then—they set the world on fire, so hot and so quick and so fucking alive. His chest aches with it—the way their spark got buried under diapers and bills and too many nights pretending they weren't lonely. He wants that fire back, but different this time. A slow burn. A fuse he's been relighting in secret.

Nate's hands are calloused from years of electrical work, and the smooth surface feels almost foreign. His grip tightens as he thinks about the journal he found a few weeks ago, tucked away on the top shelf like an explosive waiting to detonate. She labeled it Groceries 2020—because of course she did—and packed it with a hundred filthy confessions about how badly she wants him to take control again. He still can't believe those pages. That she wrote them. That she's still his.

He steps over laundry baskets on his way out of the closet, fingers clenched around the plug, his breath already catching with what's to come.

Nate takes the stairs two at a time, so eager that he almost trips. He wonders what she'll say, if she'll still blush, if she'll still get that wide-eyed look and the smallest, sexiest hitch in her breath. His pulse's a mess of anticipation by the time he reaches the kitchen and sees her standing at the sink, bathed in soft morning light.

Claire's softer now. Fuller. The kind of curves that keep a man up at night. He's never stopped wanting her, never stopped craving her, even when they fell into the kind of silence that didn't feel safe. She's putting together a sandwich, her fingers clumsy on the bread, and she doesn't see him right away.

"Hey." His voice comes out rougher than he means. Doesn't matter.

She turns, the #1 DAD mug close to her elbow, a half-empty glass of wine next to that. That chestnut hair, loose down her back—he's always loved how it looks wrapped around his fist. She looks at him, looks at what's in his hand, and he watches as her breath catches and a flush rises to her cheeks.

"You know what I've never stopped thinking about?" Nate holds up the plug, his words heavy with intent, loaded with a promise he never stopped wanting to keep.

She doesn't answer at first, but her lips part, and there's a look in her eyes that drives him wild. She's flushed and gorgeous and surprised, like he remembers her, like he dreams of her, and he wonders if she knows what she does to him. He wonders if she'll do it again.

He crosses the room, each step loud in the domestic clutter. Crayons on the floor, art projects covering the walls, a wine stain on the counter that she gave up trying to scrub. It all feels unimportant now, like background noise, like the trappings of a life he's ready to fuck her back to. He stops close enough to touch her. Doesn't. Not yet.

"Nate..." She sounds shaky. Hopeful. His pulse answers before he does.

She meets his eyes, then glances at the plug. Her tongue flicks across her bottom lip and it nearly undoes him. Almost yanks her into the laundry room and takes her like the first time—fast, dirty, the way they both need. Almost.

"Maybe this?" He dangles the toy in front of her, the barest smirk on his face. "And maybe more."

Claire lets out a breathy laugh, the kind that sounds more like a moan, and it hits him in the chest. It's enough to keep him patient. Barely.

She doesn't answer, but he sees it. The way her eyes widen, the way she nods, one silent motion that's loaded with yes, please, now. A nod that's followed by the beautiful, reckless blur of her footsteps down the hall, the space she leaves behind buzzing like a live wire.

Nate stands there, the toy still in his hand, heart pounding in anticipation and wonder. He told her once, and only once, that if she wanted him to take control, she needed to show him how much. It's been three years since she asked him like that. Three years since he knew, for sure, that she still wanted it. He's almost forgotten the feeling. Almost.

The hallway's a blur as he follows. He can't breathe right. He can't think straight. All he knows is Claire and the sound he's been dying to hear: the small, perfect click of the laundry room door locking.

The lock is flimsy, the kind you can undo with a thumbnail, but to Claire it's always meant everything. Nate steps inside and closes it. The space closes around them. Small. Familiar. Electric. He sees her leaning against the dryer like the woman he still dreams about.

Her arms are braced behind her, head tipped back in waiting, and he wants to fall to his knees, lift her tank top, mouth her bare skin and let her know how much she still owns him. How much it undoes him to see her like this, this time without hesitation. The laundry room feels untouched by the years they lost. Untouched by doubt or fear or the three sleeping babies that wedged themselves between their sheets.

"You sure you're ready for this?" he asks, knowing she is. Knowing she wouldn't be here, flushed and wanting, if she wasn't. Her response is perfect. A single nod. Then, "Are you?"

Nate laughs, low and grateful, and closes the distance between them, needing to touch her more than he needs to breathe. She's still leaning against the dryer, loose and beautiful and braless beneath her tank top. He rests his hands on her cheeks first, knowing he'll wreck her everywhere else, and Claire makes a soft, needy sound in her throat. His thumb skims her jaw, then lower, feeling her pulse, feeling her come undone for him, under him. Her hazel eyes haven't changed. Neither has that look—the one that says she trusts him to take her apart and put her back together again.

"You're fucking beautiful," he says, remembering her as the girl she used to be, loving her as the woman she is now.

He moves slowly, his hands making the trip down her body they've been aching to make since he found the plug. Her curves are fuller, her skin softer, and her nipples are hard under the loose cotton. He rolls one between his fingers, watches her arch. He could do this all day. She couldn't. Not when she's already soaked, shaking, ready for him in every way that matters.

"You really kept it?" he asks, one hand under her shirt, the other dipping low, low, lower.

Her tank top is pushed up to her chest, but Claire's voice is breathless when she answers, full of old thrill and new want. "The plug, or you?"

He makes her wait, savoring the seconds before he touches her where she needs it most. "Both," he says, slipping his hand into her pants, making her gasp like he hasn't in years.

His fingers find her slick. Ready. He presses her against the dryer like a man still fucking starved. Her hips grind forward, eager, sinful, and he closes his eyes to keep himself in check. He almost can't. Not when she's clutching his shirt, making greedy little whimpers and tugging him so hard he thinks it might tear.

"Easy, Claire." He pulls back, slides up her stomach. Watches her shudder at the loss. He doesn't miss any of it. Her half-open mouth, the tiny whimper, the way her face is flushed so deep he can practically feel it against his skin. He wants to make it worse for her, worse and better and out of her fucking mind. He wants to watch her fall apart and hear her beg for more.

His words are low, possessive. "I want to make it last."

Claire bites her lip and nods, but the message in her eyes is as loud as a scream. Please, Nate. Please, now.

He can't resist it any longer, this wife, this woman, this crazy want for both. He hauls her onto the dryer, his hands rough and reverent, and slides off her pants with the kind of control that would make her laugh if she wasn't already gasping.

He hasn't seen her like this in years. Bare. Warm. Willing. Still his. Nate runs a hand up her thigh, then lower, further, until she's soaked and open and pressing against his palm. Until her fingers twist the fabric of his shirt, pulling him to her, pulling him apart. He dips inside her again, taking his time, feeling every inch, memorizing it all.

"Still like I remember," he breathes. "Still fucking perfect."

She's squirming already, wet and wanting, and he can barely hold himself back. He adds another finger. Then another. Watches her fall apart. His whole world shrinks to this: her hips grinding for more, the sounds she makes, the way she takes him deeper.

Claire's voice is raw, begging. "God, Nate, please."

He watches her face as he moves his hand, pressure and precision, seeing how much she can take, making sure she takes everything. She's so tight around his fingers, every motion deliberate, her head tipped back and eyes closed. He can't stop staring, wondering how he got so lucky, wondering if he's already lost his mind.

"Don't worry," he says, his own voice shaking with restraint. "I've got you."

He leans down, buries his face in her neck, her hair, breathing in everything he's missed and everything she is. His words are muffled but she hears them, feels them all the way down to her trembling limbs. "I'll always have you."

She's right there, on the brink, and he doesn't know how much longer he can last before he's inside her, deep and hard and every fucking way she needs him to be. He pulls his hand away, reaching for the plug, coating it with lube, and Claire whimpers at the promise of it, her body flushed and ready for more. He moves his fingers inside her again, slow, slick strokes as he lines the toy up, feels her breath hitch as she takes it, stretches around it, breathes the sharp, sweet sounds that nearly kill him.

He withdraws and pushes back in, withdrawing and pushing until she's arching her back, matching him thrust for thrust. He doesn't let up. He doesn't fucking let go. Not even when her hands fly to his arms, fingers digging into his skin like she's close to release. Too close, because he wants her there forever.

"Don't stop, don't stop," Claire pants, her breath ragged, her body answering his in ways he never wants to forget.

He pulls the toy out with the most delicate care, sliding his fingers back inside, back into the tight heat of her pussy. The tension on her face is beautiful and erotic and drives him past the point of sense. He moves with her, so tuned to every gasp, every movement, that he doesn't realize how close he is to falling until he nearly falls apart.

"Fuck," he breathes, watching her squirm, grabbing himself and lining up before he loses the last thread of sanity. "You're so perfect, Claire."

Her legs wrap around him, dragging him closer. Nate's shaking, wrecked with want as he slips inside. He's wild with how much he loves her, how much he needs her, how she takes him in with the tightest grip and the deepest ache and the breathy sounds that keep him right on the edge.

His own voice is unsteady, barely a whisper. "I'm not gonna last."

Claire clenches around him, tighter, harder, and he moves faster, deeper, unable to stop. She's wet and gorgeous and fucking heaven, and it takes everything he has not to let go before she does.

"God, Nate, you're so…" She trails off, but he knows, he knows, and it's the knowing, as much as the feel of her, that drives him toward his breaking point.

"You're everything to me," he chokes out, his body pushed past the limits, desperate for her to come with him.

Her only answer is his name, a desperate cry and a breathless confession, as she falls apart in his arms, the sweetest thing he's ever fucking felt.

She's never looked more beautiful to him, skin flushed and soaked, his name spilling from her lips like a secret. Nate watches her as she comes, the grip of her body nearly as tight as the grip on his heart, and all the years and all the distance collapse around them until he can't hold anything back. Claire.

Their life together, trembling on the edge. Her pussy. His sanity. It's all too much, the perfect release and the need that never really left. He groans, he thrusts, and he follows her, wondering if he's ever felt so out of control and so complete.

"God, Claire." He chokes on the words as his body gives in to hers, to their past and future and the perfect right now. She's tight and soaked and holding him like he's the last thing she'll ever want, her pussy clenching around his cock, pulling him to his breaking point. She keeps his name on her lips, the sound reckless and sweet and just for him.

The orgasm is more than physical, a relief and a reckoning that shakes him to the core. He moves one last time, thrusting with everything he has, his release hot and absolute and fucking beautiful. She moans again as he spills inside her, loud and open and so undone that he nearly loses his mind. Nearly loses his grip on the dryer. Nearly loses everything but her.

He doesn't know how long they stay like that, bodies locked together, trying to catch their breath, but it doesn't feel long enough. The room is still too hot, his head still too light, the moment still too perfect when she pulls back and looks at him with those soft, hazel eyes. They say everything she doesn't. They always have.

"You okay?" Her voice is as shaky as his pulse, her legs still tight around his hips.

Nate nods, but he's not sure. Not when his body is a tangled mess of bliss and weakness and absolute worship for the woman who did this to him. Who keeps doing this to him.

"Didn't break you, did I?" Claire is flushed, smug, so fucking beautiful.

Nate pulls out gently, missing the feel of her already. The closeness, the heat, the way she fits him like she's made for it. He has to brace himself against the counter to keep from taking her again, his body a live wire of unspent want.

"I'd say you tried," he says, his voice wrecked and breathless. "Gonna have to punish you for that."

She laughs, the sound bright and clear and alive, and sits up with her feet swinging off the dryer. The edge of it is hard against her back, but Claire doesn't care. She's still on fire. She's still on the verge. She's still absolutely lost to him.

"You look pretty dead," she says, like she didn't feel him fall apart inside her. "Not sure you could even catch me if I made a run for it."

Nate raises an eyebrow, grabs her before she can move. His muscles burn, his lungs burn, but he can't let her go. Not when they're like this, sweaty and messy and brand new again. Not when her skin is bare and flushed and she's still the most tempting thing he's ever seen.

She looks up at him, sated and sleepy and so fucking trusting. It makes him want to take her all over again, slower this time, but just as thorough. It makes him want to hold her until the world ends and starts fresh with just the two of them.

"Nate…"

The way she says it, soft and deep and still wanting, gives him the strength to lift her. To keep her right where she belongs. In his arms, in his life, in his unsteady but sure-as-fuck grasp.

“Better than the dryer,” Claire murmurs against his chest, and he smiles because it’s the same thing she said the last time they locked that door.

“Always thought I was,” he says, holding her close and heading down the hall, refusing to put her down even when she swats his arm in protest.

She’s as light as his heart when they reach the bedroom, the one they painted together before their first was born. Claire’s bare feet hang against the wood floors. Her hands lace around his neck. She could run. He’d let her. But she doesn’t want to, not when this is what it feels like to stay.

“Claire,” Nate says, dropping to the edge of the bed with her. “Claire, Claire, Claire…”

“Better than the bed, too,” she whispers, smiling at the heat in his voice. She pulls him close, closer, until he’s on top of her, under her, wrapped up in everything she is.

The room is more open than the laundry space, but it feels smaller somehow. Intimate and raw and exactly what they’ve been missing. Nate remembers to breathe. Remembers to touch her. Remembers the purple candle she only lights when they’re on vacation. It burns in the corner of the room, tucked behind The Sleep Habits of Newborns and a stack of diapers they should’ve given away by now.

Nate remembers everything.

The soft curve of Claire’s mouth. The taste of salt and forgiveness on her skin. The time they were barely 20, hardly had a place of their own, and he made her come twice against the side of his pickup truck. The years they almost lost, the way they didn’t, the way he holds her now like the world has stopped and started again, the way he’s sure it will if she ever lets go.

He remembers everything. Still can’t believe she’s real.

“You’re my whole damn world,” he tells her, and means it.

Claire laughs softly, tugging him by the collar of his shirt. She’s barely keeping her eyes open. Barely keeping herself together. Barely keeping her thoughts straight when she sees the look on his face. The love, the wildness, the words she can't bear to hear in that perfect, rough voice.

"You talk too much," she says, kissing him hard and silent and sweet.

His lips are warm and possessive on hers, even when they don't move. Her laugh catches in her throat, trapped between love and air and the way they are when they're this close. Their bodies wind together, sticky with sweat and promises, their history sealed with more than words.

Nate rolls to his side, pulling her with him. "Better?" he asks, the simplest question he's asked all weekend.

"Better than anything," she answers, and the kiss she gives him tells them both what's coming.

Later, maybe next weekend, he'll open the second box. But for now, she's more than enough.

# Acknowledgments

To every thirty-something who cracked open this book between soccer drop-off and folding that same basket of laundry for the fourth time — this one's for you.

When I started writing The Laundry Room Pact, I didn't know it would become a love letter to the version of ourselves we lose in the chaos. But maybe that's the point. No one preps you for the tired, hormonal, overstimulated version of you that suddenly wakes up in your thirties — the one who can't remember the last time she felt truly seen, truly wanted, or truly like herself. I wrote this in the messy middle of figuring that out.

To my husband: thank you for loving all of me — even the wild-eyed, night-writing, sex-scene-editing goblin version. For always making me feel wanted when I felt most invisible. And for saying, "babe, do it," while at the same time mocking me for attempting to write smut.

To my friends (real and fictional): thank you for the late-night texts, the unfiltered laughter, and the kind of honesty that makes you spit wine through your nose. You reminded me that it's okay to want more—more connection, more chaos, more fun, less vanilla.

To every mom or partner or human who picked up this book and thought God, yes, this is what it's like — thank you. You are not alone. You are not broken. You are still allowed to feel wild and wanted and worthy.

And finally, to the woman I used to be — scared, tired, muted — thank you for whispering write it anyway. I'm so glad I listened.

With love and a locked laundry room door,

Nikki

After everything.

I don't know how to put this into words. Which is stupid, because I always have the words. Grocery lists. Calendars. Emergency contacts. To-do lists with bullet points so neat they could be framed.

But this? This isn't something I can check off.

We made a pact. Nate and I. A stupid, quiet, beautiful little agreement whispered next to the laundry detergent and a basket of unmatched socks. I thought maybe if we followed the rules—just like always—it would be safe. Contained. A controlled experiment in touch and memory and maybe pretending we weren't two strangers sleepwalking through marriage.

It wasn't safe.

It was real.

And I didn't know how much I missed being real. Being seen. Not just for what I do or fix or carry—but for who I am when I'm not holding everything together.

There was a moment—God, that moment—when he touched me like I was more than just the mother of his children. More than just the default setting of our house. And I didn't flinch. I leaned in.

He saw me. And I let him.

So I guess what I'm trying to say is this:

We still fold the towels. We still argue about who left the dryer lint in. We still forget things and snap and say the wrong words. But we also kiss in the hallway now. And lock the laundry room door sometimes. And look at each other like there's more to come.

I don't want perfect.

I want this. Messy, real, alive.

—Claire

# The Laundry Room Pact – Readers Guide

A Mom Club Confidential Novel
By Nikki Leigh

Discussion Questions

1. Why do you think the laundry room becomes the central seting for Claire and Nate's reconnection? How does the space reflect where their relationship is at—physically and emotionally?

2. What did you think of the "pact" Claire and Nate make to rekindle their intimacy? How do clear boundaries or intentional effort change the course of a long-term relationship?

3. Claire is deeply competent, organized, and in control—but struggling with invisible burnout. How did her emotional state resonate with you? Did you see yourself in her?

4. Nate has a quiet presence but an intense emotional undercurrent.
What makes his approach to reconnection effective—or frustrating?

5. This story is as much about emotional vulnerability as it is about sex. What moment felt like a true turning point for Claire and Nate?

6. Let's talk about the pacing. How did the slow burn and eventual release reflect the emotional journey they were on?
7. What scene felt the most tender to you? Which one felt the most raw? Were they the same?
8. The laundry room pact isn't just physical—it's emotional. What unspoken agreements do you think they were also making?
9. By the end, do you feel Claire and Nate's relationship is stronger than it was before? What work still lies ahead?
10. If you had to create a "pact" in your own relationship—what would it look like? What would your rules be?

### Bonus Prompts

- Write Your Own Pact: Emotional or physical, structured or spontaneous. What does your relationship need more of?
- Sensory Reading: Reread a key scene and notice the sensory details—touch, scent, sound. How does the domestic setting intensify the intimacy?

www.ingramcontent.com/pod-product-compliance
Ingram Content Group UK Ltd.
Pitfield, Milton Keynes, MK11 3LW, UK
UKHW010940110825
7328UKWH00035B/181

9 781997 554165